Sienna Mercer

MY SISTER THE VAMPIRE

FANGS FOR THE MEMORIES

EGMONT

With special thanks to Stephanie Burgis

For Sterrett

EGMONT
We bring stories to life

My Sister the Vampire: Fangs for the Memories! first published in
Great Britain 2016 by Egmont UK Limited, The Yellow Building,
1 Nicholas Road, London W11 4AN

Copyright © Working Partners Ltd 2016
Created by Working Partners Limited, London WC1X 9HH

ISBN 978 1 4052 7844 7

1 3 5 7 9 10 8 6 4 2

A CIP catalogue record for this title is available from the British Library

Typeset by Avon DataSet Ltd, Bidford on Avon, Warwickshire B50 4JH
Printed and bound in Great Britain by the CPI Group

60957/1

MIX
Paper
FSC   FSC® C018306

Chapter One

*U*h-oh. Ivy Vega slumped lower in her seat at the Meat and Greet as she heard a familiar voice nearby.

'Of *course* I remembered to ask for organic milk with your coffee, Tara!' Alex Shepard, a senior at Franklin Grove High, smiled sweetly at his date . . . but his fingers were drumming a telltale beat against their table.

That's such a giveaway. Ivy winced. She couldn't count how many times she'd spotted an obvious lie in the last few days. Had everyone in Franklin Grove suddenly become allergic to the truth?

Nope. Not quite everyone. Ivy relaxed as she looked

back at her identical twin sister, who sat across from her in a fluffy pink sweater and silver skirt, unhappily chopping a tofu burger into tinier and tinier pieces.

'Hey,' Ivy said. 'Are you actually going to eat that? Or are you just planning to turn it into crumbs for your new friend?' She pointed at the papier-mâché skeleton that was draped over the diner bench behind Olivia, with its skull almost propped on her shoulder.

'What?' Olivia blinked, seemingly noticing the leftover Halloween decoration for the first time. Normally it would have grossed her out completely, but now she just sighed. 'Shouldn't that have been taken down by now?'

'It has been almost a week since Halloween,' Ivy agreed.

Olivia's shoulders hunched. 'I know. And tomorrow . . .' Her green eyes filled with despair. 'Oh, Ivy. What am I going to do?'

Ivy reached across the table to take Olivia's hand, sympathy welling up inside her.

Tomorrow was the day that Jackson Caulfield, Hollywood megastar, was due to arrive in Franklin Grove – and since he was Olivia's boyfriend, that would normally be a cause for celebration. But this was to be no ordinary visit . . . not after what had happened at Halloween.

Jackson had been a crucial part of the twins' plan to chase away Gregor Gleka, TV's infamous 'Ghost Grabber', from their hometown. But Jackson was too smart not to wonder why they'd been so worried about Gleka's visit in the first place . . . He knew there was something fishy going on and had sent Olivia an email soon afterwards to ask her for an explanation. Ivy watched as her twin scrolled through Jackson's message on her phone for, like, the nineteenth time that day. By now, even Ivy knew it by heart:

3

PS: I won't ask you to do this by email, but next time I see you, I hope you'll be ready to fill me in on all the weirdness that was going on last week. I really want to understand it. XXX

'Do you think you can put him off again?' Ivy asked. 'Maybe if you say that a few of Gleka's fans are still hanging around . . .'

'I can't just keep putting him off forever.' Olivia squeezed Ivy's hand tightly in hers. 'But if I don't . . .' She dropped her voice to a whisper. 'I'll have to tell him the Blood Secret.'

It was the secret that Olivia herself had solemnly sworn to protect: that vampires were real and lived among humans.

And Ivy was one of them.

'If you tell him,' Ivy whispered back, 'you know he'll have to go through . . .' She slid her glance around the busy diner and chose her words carefully. '. . . a certain . . . *process.*'

4

She and Olivia gave identical shudders, and Ivy knew they were both remembering the Three Tests that Olivia had been forced to go through last year – to prove that, even though she was a human, she could be trusted to keep the vampires' secret.

'I'm sure . . .' Olivia paused, biting her lip. 'I *think* I'm sure Jackson could handle it. But I don't even know how to start that process.'

The papier-mâché skull shifted as someone moved further down the row of booths, until it seemed to be peering down at Olivia with hollow-eyed interest. Ivy reached out and pushed it away. 'Look,' she said quietly to her twin, 'you're going to have to take this to Dad. He'll know what to do.'

Olivia blinked rapidly, looking close to tears. 'He's going to be so angry at me!'

'Oh, Olivia.' Ivy let go of her twin's hand for just long enough to wriggle off her seat and hurry around the table. Sitting down next to Olivia, she wrapped one arm around her sister's shoulders. 'Don't worry,' she said. 'You must know Dad well enough by now to know that he won't blame you for this. He fell in love with a human, too, remember?' She tipped her head against her human sister's as she thought of the mom they'd never known. 'I don't know exactly how he'll react when he finds out about this,' she said honestly, 'but no matter what, he won't be angry. I promise.'

'I guess . . .' Olivia's shoulders rose and fell. 'But what if he demands that I stop seeing Jackson? I don't know if I can do that.'

'Let's not jump ahead of ourselves,' Ivy told her. 'We're just going to get some advice, for now. Right?'

'Right.' Olivia leaned back and closed her eyes.

Ivy's chest clenched when she saw the look on her twin's face. 'You want to tell Jackson, no matter what,' Ivy said. 'Don't you?'

Olivia opened her eyes and sat forwards again. 'I really do.' She picked up her fork as if she were finally going to eat, only to let it drop to the table straight away. 'But Ivy, even if Jackson *can* get his head around the Blood Secret . . . do you think he'd ever forgive me for lying to him about it for almost a year?' She looked miserable. 'He might break up with me.'

'Because you're being loyal to your family?' Ivy scowled. 'If he can't understand why you kept our secret, then he's not right for you.'

And that's no lie, Ivy thought.

🦇　　　🦇　　　🦇

Half an hour later Olivia was standing with Ivy outside their bio-dad's house on Undertaker Hill, shivering in the cold November wind. But it wasn't only the snow-kissed air that was sending chills through her. The big mansion at the top of Undertaker Hill had never seemed so big, so ominous, and so downright scary before.

Come on, Olivia coached herself. *This is no time to be a coward!*

Ivy put a reassuring arm around her. 'It's going to be OK. I promise.'

'Right.' Olivia took a deep breath. *I can do this!*

Squaring her shoulders, she followed Ivy through the front door and down the strangely quiet front hallway. All that Olivia could hear were the creaks and sighs of the old house's walls, with no one in sight, until Ivy pushed open the door to the kitchen.

'Hi, guys!' Their stepmom stood at the kitchen counter, smiling cheerfully as she lifted one hand to wave at the twins ... with red, gooey liquid dripping from her fingers.

'Oh, ew ... gross!' Olivia's head spun as she stumbled to a halt. 'Is that *blood?*'

'What?' Lillian blinked, then looked down at her crimson hands. 'Oh!' She laughed and grabbed a paper towel to wipe off her fingers. 'Don't worry! I'm just making raspberry jam. I've been trying out cake recipes for the big charity bake sale at Café

Creative. Remember? You guys promised to give me your opinions today.'

'Oh . . . sure! Of course.' Olivia tried to sound like her usual perky self, even though she was feeling so sick with nerves that she got a little queasy at the thought of scarfing down any sugary treats – especially blood-coloured ones! But a promise was a promise, so she forced herself to nod, even as she braced herself for something that she wanted even less. 'Is . . . is Dad around?'

'I'm right here.' Charles spoke just behind her, and Olivia jumped. He stood in the kitchen doorway, looking as elegant and formal as usual in a well-tailored black suit and tie. But as she spun around to face him, his eyebrows lowered into a concerned frown. 'Olivia, what's wrong?'

'I . . .' She swallowed hard. She knew she had to tell him the truth. She *knew* it! But now that the moment had actually come her chest felt so tight she didn't know how she could ever squeeze out the words.

Charles nodded gravely, his eyes fixed on her face. 'I can see that there's something you need to talk about.'

'What is it, sweetheart?' Lillian's voice was warm.

'I think . . .' Olivia forced out a thin whisper. 'I think, maybe, you two should sit down for this.'

'All right.' Charles nodded to Ivy, who was hovering by the kitchen door and looking worried. 'I can tell that this is serious.' He sat down next to Lillian at the breakfast bar and patted the tall chair beside him for Olivia. Obediently, she sat down . . . but when she opened her mouth, nothing came out.

I can't do it. Shivers rippled up and down her body as she looked at her bio-dad's expectant face.

It had taken her so long to finally meet him – and even longer to really get to know him. Now that she did, his opinion, and his respect, had come to mean so much to her. How was he going to feel when he found out that she wanted to reveal his most important secret to a human outsider?

And what would he think of her?

'Olivia.' Charles gave her a slight smile, as if saying that whatever she wanted to tell him was going to be fine.

Ivy stepped up behind her and set her hand on Olivia's arm. Lillian's expression was full of concern.

Surrounded by her vamp family, Olivia closed her eyes and nodded to herself. *Time to tell them everything.* 'So, you know how freaked out the whole vamp community got when Gregor Gleka came to town?'

'Mm-hmm.' Charles nodded, his expression unreadable.

Olivia waited hopefully . . . but he didn't speak again. *Why can't he just figure it out from that?* she thought miserably. It would be so much easier if he just put the pieces together so she didn't have to say it out loud . . .

But if he had figured it out, he didn't give it away with so much as a blink, so she forced herself onwards. 'And . . . you know how we got Jackson to come in and distract everyone?'

'Yes.' Charles nodded again. 'He used his "Chatter" account, too, didn't he?'

Behind Olivia, Ivy gave a muffled snort. 'You mean "Twitter", Dad.'

Charles shrugged. 'Whatever you call it,' he said, 'Jackson spreading the word about Gleka's "hoax" certainly helped convince the world that there was nothing of supernatural interest in Franklin Grove – no ghosts, and no vampires. He did us a huge favour, without even knowing it.'

'Well . . .' Olivia gripped the counter of the breakfast bar with both hands. 'He may have helped us to fool everyone else . . . but he's finally figured out for himself that there *is* something very strange about this town . . .' Her voice rose to a near-squeak: 'And he wants to know what it is!'

She snapped her mouth shut, bracing for her bio-dad's reaction.

'Hmm.' Charles traded a long glance with Lillian. When he finally turned back to Olivia, his voice was quiet and controlled. 'You don't want to lie to him any more, do you?'

'No,' Olivia admitted. 'I really don't. But . . .' Her fingers tightened around the counter. If only she could read his expression! She couldn't even tell whether he was angry or not. 'More than anything else,' she went on, 'I really, *really* don't want to put you guys at risk! I just don't know what to do.'

'You'll need to think long and hard about telling Jackson the truth,' Charles told her. 'Even I don't know what the rules are about a human revealing the Blood Secret to another human. When I married your mother, Susannah and I went into hiding rather than try to go through the Three

13

Tests ourselves. But that's not an option for you.'

'No,' Olivia agreed softly. As the lead actress in one of the biggest upcoming movies in the world – and the girlfriend of Hollywood's biggest teen movie star – invisibility was not an option for her.

Charles drummed his fingers on the breakfast bar, lips pursed as he thought things through. 'I'll do some research into the matter,' he said. 'But now, I believe we have no choice but to bring this to the attention of the Vampire Round Table. I can't tell you what they'll say about it, because I've never been in this situation before.'

'But they did let you guys tell *me* the truth,' Olivia said hopefully.

'Yes, but you were told the secret by your vampire sister and father,' Lillian said gently. 'This time it would be a human vouching for Jackson, not a vampire.'

'And . . .' Charles winced. '. . . I'm afraid they won't like that at all.'

14

His expression turned grim as he looked back at Olivia. 'Even if you are granted permission, you know that Jackson will still have to undergo the Three Tests required of non-vampires, to prove to the Vampire Round Table that he can be trusted.'

'And if he fails,' Lillian added softly, 'he'll have his memory erased. You do understand that, don't you?'

How could I not? Olivia asked herself, remembering the threat of the memory-erasing concoction 'offered' by the Round Table. It had looked so much like a strawberry smoothie that, ever since, she had always been a little bit wary whenever she ordered one in Mister Smoothie's.

Charles leaned forwards, the most seriously serious look on his face. 'All traces of you, and even of Franklin Grove, will be deleted from his memory. That means, as far as Jackson is concerned, you will never have been a couple at all.'

Olivia's stomach clenched. Everything she

and Jackson had shared over the last year flashed through her mind. The kisses, the fun, the adventure, the warmth . . .

Even just working together on the two movies they'd made had been some of the best times of her entire . . . 'Wait!' she said. 'Can the vampires really erase *The Groves* and *Eternal Sunset* from existence?' She shook her head in confusion. 'Would they have to erase the memories of everyone who saw them, too? That's, like, millions of people! What are they going to do, confiscate all the DVDs of *The Groves* and then dump them?'

'Um . . .' Ivy began.

But Olivia was too panicked to slow down. 'I can't believe it!' she said. 'Not only could the vamps completely erase my relationship, they could also damage the whole *environment*!' She gestured so wildly, she nearly fell off the chair. 'Who knew that me having a boyfriend could hurt the whole *world*?'

'Olivia!' Ivy's hands grabbed her arms, breaking

through her daze. 'Calm down! You're having a panic attack!'

Oops. Olivia forced herself to take a deep breath as she saw the wide-eyed way her whole vamp family was staring at her.

'Sorry,' she mumbled. 'I guess I . . . kind of freaked out, didn't I?'

'That's OK,' Lillian said. 'We understand. Just try to relax.'

'But you're right about the problem presented by your movies,' Charles said, staring at the wall as if thinking hard. 'I admit, I hadn't thought about that part. Perhaps we'd better reach out to the VRT and ask *all* of these questions before we even begin to think about how to present any of this to Jackson.' He looked back to Olivia, still seriously serious. 'At the moment, all we can do is keep the VRT fully informed . . . for everyone's sake.'

'Right.' Olivia should have been worried by her father's straight face and grave tone, but she was actually starting to calm down. If Charles and Lillian weren't freaking out, then there was no reason for her to. She slipped off her stool. 'We'll play this by the book and we'll totally fix everything,' she said. Then she shrugged. 'Just as soon as we figure out exactly *what* we're going to do.'

'Yes.' Rising to his feet, Charles wrapped his arms around Olivia in a warm and uncharacteristic hug. 'Everything's going to be fine.' His breath ruffled her hair. 'You've done the right thing in being honest, and I'm proud of you.'

'Thanks, Dad.' Olivia felt her muscles start to relax as she leaned into his hug . . . but then she looked over his shoulder and saw the concerned expression on Lillian's face.

Of course, she realised. *I may be playing by the vampires' rules . . . but that still doesn't mean that Jackson is safe.*

Chapter Two

Before she knew it, Olivia was walking with Ivy and their bio-dad through the ominous-looking iron security gate that the headquarters of ASHH – The Agency for the Security of Human Hybrids. Olivia shivered as she looked at the hulking black glass building ahead of them. It glistened like a dark jewel, sucking in all of the pale November sunlight and bringing back far too many bad memories. It had been a year since she'd last come here, but she still wasn't nearly ready to come back.

This is for Jackson, she told herself. *And for an honest relationship – the kind he deserves.*

Steeling herself, she stepped through the front door of the building and crossed the cavernous black marble lobby to the elevator, holding her head high.

Unfortunately when she stepped out of the elevator with her family a minute later she was met by a scarily familiar face. Frankie – the ridiculously tall security guard who had come into conflict with her and Ivy a year ago – was standing next to the office door, directly in front of the dark wall that read 'ASHH' in glowing letters. *Uh-oh. I really hope he's forgotten us by now.*

Frankie turned to look at them. His eyes flared wide. 'You!'

Guess not. Olivia winced – obviously, he remembered only too well the way that she and Ivy had tricked him into getting locked on the wrong side of a fire door during their first visit.

'What are you two doing here?' Frankie demanded.

20

Olivia took an involuntary step backwards, but Ivy didn't even look nervous. 'We have an appointment,' she said breezily. 'So if you wouldn't mind . . .?' She raised her eyebrows as she pointed expectantly at the door beside him.

'Yeah, right.' Frankie scoffed and crossed his arms. 'Like I'd believe anything you two troublemakers told me!'

'Ahem.' Behind Ivy, Charles let out a low cough. 'The girls are with me today, Frankie . . . and we really can't be late for this appointment.'

'Fine.' The security guard scowled. 'But you'd better keep a good eye on them!'

He stepped aside, but Olivia sensed his fierce glare against her back as she passed through the door.

'I don't want any drama this time!' he called after them.

Neither do I, Olivia thought unhappily.

The office beyond was still filled with the

same rows of desks she remembered from last time, but now – as this was an official visit rather than sneaking in after working hours – dozens of vampires were sitting hunched over desktop computers. Most were as ancient as Olivia had expected, but some more modern devices had also been added to the mix. Raising her eyebrows, Ivy gestured at a new-looking tablet on the corner of a desk as they passed. 'Hey, ASHH is actually moving with the times!'

'Shh.' Charles gave her a quelling look as he led the way across the office. 'Remember, everyone who works here can hear you no matter how quietly you speak.'

'Whoops.' Ivy shrugged, still smiling. 'Where are we going, anyway?'

Charles pointed at the door ahead of them. 'A representative of the Vampire Round Table is waiting for us in Meeting Room A to discuss our . . . problem.'

Olivia's chest tightened. 'Could we please not call Jackson a "problem"?' she asked.

Her father gave her a grave look but didn't reply. Instead, he raised his hand and knocked firmly on the meeting room door.

'Enter!' called a too-familiar voice.

Oh, stake me now! Olivia thought, borrowing a phrase from her goth sister's vocabulary in her dismay. *Not her again!*

As Olivia walked into the dark grey room, her gaze went straight to the tall woman in a striking black and red kimono who stood at the far end of a long wooden table. Valencia Deborg, Secretary of Human Relations for the VRT, obviously hadn't bothered to put in her contact lenses that morning . . . and her fiery red vampire eyes were focused directly on Olivia.

She was not exactly over the moon when I passed my Tests last year, Olivia thought. *I don't think she approves of* any *human knowing the Blood Secret.*

23

That was why it was such a surprise when Ms Deborg gave a small smile as she gestured to Olivia and her family. 'You'd better all take a seat.' She smoothed down her kimono as she sat down herself, then gave a light laugh. 'Well! When this young lady was first brought to the Round Table's attention last year . . .' She pointed to Olivia, and her long blood-red-painted fingernails glinted in the light. '. . . I thought *her* circumstances were the most exceptional I'd ever heard. But I think this new little drama might just top it!'

Olivia smiled uncomfortably. Suddenly she knew why Ms Deborg was smiling – she was enjoying the fact that the bunny who passed the Tests was now in a different sticky situation.

Then Ms Deborg's smile disappeared. 'Now, Charles, do you finally understand why we must *all* be so strict about keeping the Blood Secret? First, we agree to tell one human . . . and then it spirals! How many more humans will find out about us simply because we agreed to trust your daughter?'

Olivia hunched her shoulders, but her father was not rising to Ms Deborg's taunt. 'This was not a result of carelessness on anyone's part,' he said quietly. 'It could not have been helped.'

'You think not?' Ms Deborg snorted. 'Are we to go through this rigmarole every time your daughter has a crush?' She spat out the last word as if it was rotten food on her tongue.

The noise charged out of Olivia's mouth almost without her control. A gasp, and a huff. She shook her head, until she noticed the secretary staring right at her, an enigmatic smile on her face. 'Do you have something you wish to say?' she asked.

Olivia made an effort not to look away. 'I'm not a silly kid,' she said. 'I wouldn't volunteer Jackson for this if I didn't expect him to pass.'

Ms Deborg gave a single nod of the head. 'I can certainly see that *your* feelings run deep. I only hope, for your sake, that young Mr Caulfield's feelings match them. Now . . .' She opened the dark red ring binder that sat on the table in front of her. 'As you may recall from our last discussion, the original tests set to determine whether or not a human could be trusted to keep the Blood Secret were torturous, hideous, and . . .' Her smile deepened. '. . . excruciatingly painful. Failure to pass them inevitably resulted in death for the nominated subject. But!' Her eyes narrowed, and her smile vanished, her voice sounding annoyed. 'Since the 1926 Vampiric Accord, the tests have been downgraded. The price of failure nowadays is minimal – a simple strawberry concoction that washes away dangerous memories, for everyone's protection.'

Not so simple for Jackson. Olivia traded a look with her father, who sat on her left. From the frown on his face she knew he too was thinking about the problem of wiping her from Jackson's memory, with two major Hollywood movies available to show him the truth.

'Of course . . .' Ms Deborg gave a rueful smile. 'That procedure will do no good in this instance. So the rules will have to be a little different.'

'How different?' Olivia's fingers curled together in her lap. 'If Jackson failed, what would happen to him?'

'Well . . .' The secretary flipped through the pages of her binder, then turned it around. 'What do you think of this as an explanation?'

Olivia's eyes widened in horror.

A picture of a heart filled the page . . . but something was very wrong with it. Most of the heart was blood red, but the bottom edge had been coloured pitch black, and the blackness seemed to be creeping upward, ready to swallow up the rest.

Her voice emerged as a panicked squeak. 'What does that *mean*?'

'It means,' Ms Deborg responded calmly, 'that we may not be able to simply erase Jackson's memory – but what we *can* do is Darken his heart.'

A sharp intake of breath sounded on Olivia's left and she jerked around, her throat closing up. *Oh no.* She'd never heard her perfectly controlled bio-dad gasp like that before. If even he was scared by this . . .

She forced the words out of her too-tight throat. 'What is she talking about?'

Charles's jaw flexed – he looked a little tense. This made Olivia feel even more nervous. 'If Jackson's heart is Darkened, Olivia,' he said, 'it means that his love for you will die. He will remember your time together . . . but not fondly.' He shook his head, his dark eyes filled with sadness. 'Jackson may well think of you as someone who was mean to him on movie sets, whom he did his best to avoid.'

'What?' Olivia stared at her father, dizziness threatening to overwhelm her. 'But . . . that's *horrible!*'

It had been terrible enough to imagine that

Jackson might not even remember that they'd ever met . . . but to have him remember all their time together as *bad*? To think of her as *mean*?

Olivia slumped backwards in her chair, her stomach clenching uncomfortably. If strawberry smoothies were what the vamps used to erase memories, what flavour would they use to Darken hearts? Raspberry or blackcurrant, she guessed.

'I . . . I don't know if I can cope with Jackson remembering me as someone he didn't care about.'

'Oh no?' Ms Deborg's voice was cold, almost bored-sounding. When Olivia turned she found the secretary frowning at her. 'Sounds like you don't have all that much faith in your little human boyfriend after all.'

Argh. Olivia jerked up her chin, forcing her shoulders to straighten as anger overcame her panic. 'Of *course* Jackson can pass the trials,' she said. 'And he *can* keep the secret. I don't care what the punishment for failure would be, because he won't fail. I vouch for him!'

'You can't vouch for him.' Ms Deborg's made a face like she was mildly irritated Olivia had even assumed she could. 'You're not one of us, and *that's* what makes this situation so . . . unconventional.'

'Fine.' Ivy leaned forwards, her jaw stuck out at a stubborn angle. 'I'll totally vouch for Jackson. I'm a vamp – so, problem staked, right?'

But Olivia could hear a telltale wobble in her twin's voice. *Even Ivy isn't sure he'll pass!* Although the fact that Ivy would vouch for him anyway, for Olivia's sake, was incredibly sweet . . .

Ms Deborg didn't seem to think so. She pursed her lips, looking at Ivy with irritation. 'Unfortunately,' she snapped, 'this is an *even more* exceptional set of circumstances than your last request. Vampire lore states that it must be she or he who wishes to share the secret who provides the guarantee, and – this time – it is a human . . . It's unheard of.'

'Then what *can* we do?' Olivia demanded. 'If you won't let anyone vouch for him, how are you ever going to decide whether he can undergo the Tests?'

'We must approach this in a different way.' Ms Deborg slammed her binder shut. 'I suggest, preliminary trials!' she announced. 'We will give your Jackson a set of early, *easy* challenges. Only if he passes them will the Vampire Round Table consider him fit for the real Tests.'

'Seriously?' Olivia dug her fingers into the table, fighting to keep her expression polite. 'Preliminary trials, and *then* the actual Tests? How is that even slightly fair to Jackson?'

She expected the secretary to lecture her for her tone. Instead – and even more frighteningly – Ms Deborg just stared at her, her face as still and expressionless as a mannequin's.

'Jackson will have help,' the secretary said. 'He is not be the only one about to be tested.'

How do I make a salad AND cross all my fingers? Ivy wondered the next morning.

She was standing in Olivia's kitchen, helping Mrs Abbott prepare lunch, but she couldn't stop fidgeting with her baseball cap . . . and thinking about Olivia. At that very minute, her twin was being taken to ASHH HQ for her preliminary interview about her relationship with Jackson. If that didn't go well . . .

It will be fine, Ivy told herself. *Olivia is totally going to nail it – I know she will!*

'Olivia, sweetheart,' Mrs. Abbott said, 'I don't think you can chop those onions any finer without making them disappear! Why don't you wash some lettuce for me instead?'

'Oops.' With a guilty smile, Ivy dropped her kitchen knife and accepted the colander full of lettuce from her twin's adoptive mom. 'Sorry about that.'

'It's OK.' Mrs Abbott dropped a kiss on her head. 'I know you're excited about seeing Jackson today.'

'Um ... yeah. Right. Of course.' Ivy swallowed hard.

Ivy had her own part to play in the first of three preliminary trials Jackson had to pass before he would be allowed to take the Tests to prove he could keep the Blood Secret. She was dressed in clothes from Olivia's closet – a loosely draped glittering pink sweater over trim silver trousers – and had scrubbed off all the dark kohl from around her eyes. With her sister's favourite bright pink lipstick sparkling on her lips and her own goth clothes hidden underneath Olivia's bed, there was nothing left to distinguish vamp Ivy from her bunny twin. Even Mr and Mrs Abbott hadn't realised that they'd swapped places!

I hope Jackson's more observant than the Abbotts, Ivy thought, feeling a tingle of worry in her chest. *Because if* he *thinks I'm Olivia, he will fall at the VRT's first hurdle.*

Cold water ran over Ivy's fingers as she washed the lettuce, but she barely noticed. She was too busy stewing over the way Valencia Deborg had announced her so-called 'official' preliminary trials to test her sister's relationship. *Considering she was still busy thinking them up until the ending of our meeting, I don't think they really count as official . . . just mean!*

The VRT seemed determined to drive a wedge between Olivia and Jackson, just to keep their secret safe. *It's so unfair!* Ivy gritted her teeth, only dimly aware that she was mangling the lettuce in her hands. Olivia and Jackson had worked so hard to be together, but now Olivia was facing the prospect of losing him to protect her family . . . *What kind of choice is that?*

She startled out of her thoughts as Mr Abbott,

who was busy setting the table, called across to his wife. 'Honey? Where did you put the homewares catalogue I was looking at last week?'

'You had a catalogue?' The tone of Mrs Abbott's voice made Ivy's vamp senses jangle. Olivia's adoptive mom had a naturally sweet cheerful voice, but as she spoke now Ivy sensed a disconcerting thrumming sound behind her words, like an engine revving. What could it mean? 'I haven't s-seen it,' Mrs Abbott said, turning away from her husband to lean over her chopping board. 'Have you ch-checked in the living room?'

Ivy frowned. Mrs Abbott's voice was kind of quivering, and she seemed to be holding on to her vowels like they were precious to her. She was lying to her husband – but why?

Ding-dong!

The doorbell rang, and Ivy jumped so suddenly she sent a blizzard of lettuce flying through the air.

Thank darkness for vamp reflexes! She saved the

salad just in time, her arms moving almost too quickly to be seen . . . then winced. *Oops. Hope no one noticed that . . .*

'Well caught,' said Mr Abbott, as he stepped into the kitchen. 'Your cheerleading days certainly gave you good reflexes, Olivia. But then, "Fletchers shape the arrow shaft, carpenters shape the wood, and the wise control themselves," right?'

'Um . . . maybe?' Ivy had never really known how to respond to Mr Abbott's aphorisms. But she didn't have time to worry about that now . . . because she knew exactly who had rung the doorbell.

With Jackson waiting at the door, it was time for Ivy to play the actress in the family!

'Well, dear?' Mrs Abbott looked at her expectantly. 'Aren't you going to go let him in?'

Ivy thought fast. There was no reason for 'Olivia' to not go and greet her boyfriend at the door — but 'Olivia' always greeted Jackson with a kiss-hello ... and there was *no way* that Ivy was about to do that! If 'Olivia' refused to kiss Jackson, he would know instantly that something was up, and would start asking questions, and the whole preliminary trial could fall apart before it had even got started ... The VRT had made it very clear that Ivy was to do her absolute best impression of Olivia; because, if she looked – and acted – *exactly* like her twin, and Jackson was *still* able to tell the difference, that would be a sign that he really did know her.

'It will show that his heart "sings" to hers,' Ms Deborg had said, the sarcasm in her voice so strong Ivy felt like it was hitting her in the face.

There was only one thing for it – stalling. 'No can do,' she said, laughing weakly as she raised her dripping wet hands from the colander. 'Right now, all my love is going on this lettuce.'

'Olivia?' Mrs Abbott frowned. 'Is something wrong? Usually, you'd be flying to the door.'

'Um . . .' *Oh garlic salt!* Of course she ought to be acting giddy with excitement. It was 'Olivia's' first time seeing her boyfriend in nearly a week!

Maybe stress can sound giddy, too. Ivy hoped so, as she forced a pained grin. 'I just really, really want his salad to be absolutely *perfect*!'

The doorbell rang again and Mrs Abbott chuckled. 'I'm pretty sure Jackson is here for you, not for the food, dear.' But her footsteps moved off towards the door and Ivy let out a muffled sigh of relief as she bent over her chore.

These were going to be the cleanest lettuce leaves *ever*!

Behind her, she heard a disapproving cough from her sister's adoptive dad. 'You know, Olivia, "the hand that turns to the task has no gender." The fact that you happen to be a girl doesn't mean you need to take on a domestic role in your relationship.'

'I know, Dad.' Ivy raised an eyebrow. 'Don't

worry!' Mr Abbott might think he was talking to Olivia, but the answer would have been the same no matter which twin he was speaking to.

There is no chance of either of us ever agreeing to do all the housework!

'Hey, guys!' Jackson stepped into the kitchen, beaming his famous megawatt smile. 'I have gifts for everyone!' He hoisted a heavy-looking shopping bag in one hand and handed it to Mr Abbott. 'A Buddhist water feature for you, sir. A scarf for you, Mrs Abbott . . . and Olivia . . .' He stepped closer, his grin turning wry as behind him the two adults exclaimed over their gifts. Jackson was holding up a Manila envelope with 'MISS ABBOTT' written on it in Sharpie. '. . . gets the best gift of all. Revised sides for our next scenes in *Eternal Sunset*.'

What in the name of darkness are 'revised sides'? Ivy wondered. *How do you 'revise' a side?* 'That's . . . great!' she said, and tried to inject as much perky cheerfulness as she could into her tone.

Jackson's eyebrows drew together in a frown. 'Um . . . seriously?' he asked.

'Of course.' Ivy gave him her best cheery-bunny smile. 'Thanks for bringing them!'

'Ohh-kay . . .' He shook his head, eyeing her warily. 'Well, this is unprecedented. You usually freak out whenever scenes get rewritten. And this is, like, the fifth time we've gotten revised sides so far, right?'

Oops! My bad. Ivy shrugged, trying to look blasé. 'I guess I'm just used to upheaval by now.'

'Right,' Jackson said. But his frown didn't entirely disappear.

Don't panic, Ivy told herself, because she was kind of beginning to panic. *You can do this. You know Olivia almost as well as you know yourself!*

'Come on, dear.' Mrs Abbott waved her hands at her husband. 'Let's put away our gifts and give the children a moment to say hello before lunch

40

begins. Jackson, sweetheart? Will you help Olivia get a start on the cake we'll be eating after lunch?'

'Of course,' Jackson said. He smiled at Ivy. 'We've always been a good baking team, haven't we?'

Code red! More panic rippled up Ivy's spine as the older Abbotts left the room, smiling and closing the kitchen door behind them . . . and leaving Ivy completely alone with her sister's boyfriend.

. . . who would definitely expect a kiss.

This can't happen! Think, Vega – think!

As Jackson stepped towards her, Ivy did a quick sidestep, grabbing a mixing bowl and a carton of eggs like she was about to take them into battle. 'I guess we'd better get started!' Her voice sounded bright and brittle to her own ears . . . and more than a little *desperate*.

Please don't try to kiss me! Please, please, please . . .

Ivy was supposed to do everything that Olivia would do in this situation. But if she did . . .

She cringed at the thought.

Darkness, how many girls around the world would love to have this 'problem' right now? 'Oh no, Jackson Caulfield wants to kiss me!'

Besides, Jackson might be gorgeous by bunny standards, with his shining blond hair and bright blue eyes, but Ivy happened to be dating a boy who exactly fit her definition of 'perfect'. With his floppy black hair and sweet lopsided grin, Brendan was her ideal match . . . and oh, no, she just couldn't kiss another boy.

I can't do it to Brendan – and I can't do it to Olivia! This is too weird . . .

She ducked her head over her mixing bowl and started working on the eggs, her whisk whirling madly through the yellowy liquid.

'Wow,' Jackson said, directly behind her. 'You're really giving those eggs a beating. What did they ever do to you?'

Bracing herself, Ivy turned to look over her shoulder at him . . . and found him grinning at her, his eyes sparkling with mischief. 'OK, Ivy,' he said. 'Tell the truth. What kind of prank are you two playing now?'

Oh thank darkness! Ivy grinned in relief. 'It's not a prank,' she said hastily. 'Olivia had to go off with Charles to, uh, shop for an anniversary gift for the Abbotts, and she didn't want them to guess what she was doing. That's all.' It wasn't even a total lie, she reassured herself. After all, Olivia and Charles *would* be doing that . . . right after their meeting with the VRT!

'OK.' Jackson shrugged and started measuring out flour into another mixing bowl. 'Just don't get *too* comfortable with the switcheroos, all right? You don't want to forget you're Ivy, not Olivia!'

'Ha!' Ivy shook her head. 'There's no chance of that happening.' *And pretty soon, you'll know exactly what I mean when I say that!* For the first time that morning she gave her twin's boyfriend a real smile. 'So how did you know I wasn't Olivia in the first place?'

Jackson gave her a long look. 'Do you really think I don't know my own girlfriend?' He shook his head. 'For one thing, when Olivia beats eggs, she *always* uses a clockwise motion. You were beating your eggs counter-clockwise.'

'I was?' Ivy blinked down at the eggs she was beating . . . and realised he was right. 'Even I didn't know that I did that!'

'Mm-hmm.' Jackson nodded, his lips twitching. 'And you might be wearing Olivia's make-up, but no amount of make-up can change your . . . oh, let's call it your *less sunny* disposition?'

'Very funny.' Ivy scowled at him.

'You see?' He laughed and pointed at her scowling face. 'I rest my case!'

'Hmmph.' Ivy fake-punched his arm. 'Watch out, buster, or I'm going to tell your girlfriend you've been mean to me!'

As they settled into their job, working companionably side by side at the kitchen counter, she had to look away from him so that he didn't see the relieved smile that broke out on her face. He'd definitely have more questions if he saw. Ivy couldn't help it, though.

She quickly dried her hands and ducked out into the corridor to text Olivia. *Jackson totally staked the first test!*

As she heard the *whoosh* of her message being sent, Ivy remembered: there were still two more to come . . . The VRT seemed determined to put a lot of red tape in front of Jackson.

Ivy just hoped he didn't trip over any of it . . .

Chapter Three

*O*K, *well,* this *is creepy − even by Franklin Grove standards!*

Olivia was sitting at the same meeting table in ASHH headquarters where her family had met with Valencia Deborg the day before; but this time, she was all on her own with the intimidating VRT secretary . . . and they were watching a movie of Olivia's life on the massive projector screen that had unscrolled to cover one full wall of the meeting room.

Her stomach churned with outrage that the VRT had been taping her day after day, because that was *such* an invasion of privacy. Then she could not help wondering if they had footage from her English class last year, when she was sat next to a nasty vampire boy called Garrick Stephens, who 'miraculously' got the same score as her on the test that they took.

She was *sure* that he copied her answers.

'And now . . .' Ms Deborg glanced down at her tablet as footage from the Franklin Grove Middle School's production of *Romezog and Julietron* played across the screen. 'Let's see some surveillance footage from your London trip.' She tapped a button on the tablet and the screen shifted.

Suddenly the roofs and spires of London scrolled across the screen, while on the busy street below . . .

Olivia couldn't help but smile as she recognised that moment: running side by side with Jackson through the streets, fleeing the hordes of teenage girls who'd been chasing him.

It really was fun, wasn't it? It had been such an odd

moment in their relationship, but now that she and Jackson were so solidly together again the memory of that day filled her with nostalgic warmth . . . despite the total creepiness of knowing that the VRT had been filming them the entire time!

The footage of them running was replaced by photos of them standing in the Globe Theatre, holding hands for the first time in months as they'd watched a performance of *Romeo and Juliet* – the real play, not her friend Camilla's intergalactic reimagining. Jackson's mouth was open, caught in the middle of speaking the lines along with the actor on stage . . .

Hey, wait. Olivia straightened in her seat, taking a closer look. From the angle of that photo . . .

'That picture was taken *from* the stage,' she gasped. She swivelled around to stare at Ms Deborg. 'Are you telling me that a member of the cast or crew at the Globe Theatre was actually a spy for the Vampire Round Table?'

Ms Deborg gave an elegant shrug. 'I can neither confirm nor deny that speculation,' she said coolly. 'The VRT takes secrecy *very* seriously, as you should have gathered by this point.' She tapped another button on her tablet and the footage on-screen froze. 'Now.' Her eyes narrowed. 'It's time to begin the next stage of Jackson's preliminary trials ... and this one will be won or lost by *you*.'

She opened a massive ring binder. 'I cannot stress enough, this is a most *unprecedented* situation. A human vouching for another human – and every vampire knows that humans are creatures driven more by emotions than logic. For this reason, we have to consider your request to be a potentially huge risk to our security, and it is *absolutely essential* that we test both of you thoroughly and rigorously. It's time to find out how well you *really* know your boyfriend.'

Olivia bit down hard on her tongue to hold back

the response she wanted to make: *you said you wanted to test how strong my relationship with Jackson is — surely, giving away secrets isn't 'strong'. This test is designed for me to fail!*

But Ms Deborg had already raised a quill pen, looking at Olivia with icy disdain. 'Now, then, first question: which of his teeth did Jackson chip in a baseball accident when he was eight?'

Olivia's eyes widened. *How on earth did she find out about that?* Jackson had had his teeth professionally fixed years ago and he'd never, ever told the story of his broken tooth in any interviews or news stories. Only a few people in the world had ever heard about it . . . and in the heat of the moment, with Ms Deborg's penetrating gaze piercing through her, Olivia found her mind going blank.

Think, think, think!

Squeezing her eyes shut, she desperately tried to remember. She'd seen an old family photo once of an eight-year-old Jackson grinning with a broken tooth . . . but which tooth had it been?

She drew a slow, deep breath, drawing on the memorisation skills she'd learned in her acting career. *Let the image come . . .*

Relaxing her shoulders, she visualised young Jackson with a broken right canine . . . but even as the image formed, it suddenly warped, switching the break to his left front tooth . . . then his right incisor. *Argh!* She just couldn't be sure. But she had to say something!

Olivia opened her eyes and hoped for the best. 'His right canine,' she said firmly.

'Hmm.' Ms Deborg's lips pinched as if she'd bitten into a lemon. 'That is correct,' she muttered. 'But that was only the beginning. Now you need to tell me: what is Jackson's mother's middle name?'

Oh thank goodness – something I definitely know. 'Catherine,' Olivia said.

She relaxed even more as the questions continued, each of them easy and familiar, until . . .

'Now!' Ms Deborg's eyes narrowed and her quill pen hovered above her file. 'Tell me, young lady: what are your boyfriend's deepest phobias and fears?'

Wow. Olivia's eyebrows rose. *If they've found out about those out too, the VRT really must have a long reach!*

Jackson only had a few phobias, but he kept them super-*super*-secret! Still, at least this was another question she could easily answer. She ticked the points off on her fingers as she spoke. 'He doesn't like being in total darkness,' she began. 'That's the problem with having a creative imagination – far too easy to imagine all sorts of scary monsters lurking in the shadows!' Olivia laughed, but Ms Deborg didn't. She almost seemed incapable. 'Also, he's been weirded out by clowns ever since he had a bad experience at a birthday party when he was little, and he *really* has a thing about mice and rats.'

There. She looked expectantly at the VRT

secretary, who had scribbled notes all through her speech.

'Hmm.' Ms Deborg set down her quill and sat back in her chair. 'You got every question right,' she said icily.

Whew! Olivia smiled. *I guess I* really *know my bf!*

But the secretary's red eyes narrowed. 'It seems,' she said, 'that Mr Caulfield is quite the open book. If he hasn't managed to keep any of those secrets from you, then what exactly makes you think he can be trusted with the vampires' secret?'

Olivia shook her head in disbelief. Wasn't it obvious? 'Because he loves me.'

'How . . . sweet.' Ms Deborg's upper lip curled disdainfully. 'There is one piece of Hollywood gossip that Jackson does not seem to have shared with you, though. Did you know that your boyfriend's colleague Keith Carter has been lying about some of his skills?'

Olivia blinked at the sudden change in topic.

I feel like I've got conversational whiplash!

'Um, I'm sorry?' she said finally. She knew the eighteen-year-old actor's name – she'd even met him a couple of times, when he'd visited the set of *Eternal Sunset* – but she couldn't imagine what Ms Deborg was talking about.

The secretary continued. 'Mr Carter once told a director he was fluent in Russian in order to win a role in an action film. Unfortunately, his accent was so appalling he had to have all of his dialogue dubbed in post-production.' She shook her head gently. 'And I think young Mr Carter's fans would be most upset to learn that all of those complicated dance moves that he *apparently* pulled off in his last musical were actually performed by a secret stunt double! Once again, Mr Carter had lied to the director about his own skills in order to win the role.'

'No!' Olivia gasped. 'That can't be right.' She stared at the secretary, horrified. Keith had seemed like such a nice guy every time she'd talked to him. He couldn't be the liar that Ms Deborg was describing! But then she knew only too well the pressures of Hollywood. It would be easy to get sucked into exaggerating your skills to keep your career on track.

'Oh come now, Olivia – you can hardly be surprised.' Ms Deborg waved a dismissive hand, her blood-red fingernails glistening in the office's fluorescent light. 'It's show business we're talking about, remember? No one is honest . . . and *no one* can be trusted. Not even your beloved boyfriend.' She leaned forwards, pushing her binder aside. 'And *that* is how we've decided on his next pre-trial. Later today, you will do everything you can to get Jackson to break Keith's confidence. Let's see what means more to Mr Caulfield – his girlfriend, or his word.'

She gave a smile that made Olivia shiver. 'If he so much as *hints* about the truth – even without naming Keith as the actor who did it – then that will tell us all we need to know.'

Olivia's head swam, her stomach clenching with dread. *So, if Jackson takes me into his confidence, he* fails*?!*

Four hours later, Olivia sat waiting for Jackson in the Franklin Grove mall, the butterflies in her stomach going haywire. It was the first time she'd seen him since just after Halloween, and she knew he would be expecting answers about all the weird things that had been happening then. But she couldn't give him any until he'd passed all of his pre-trials . . . and this was going to be the hardest one yet.

As her gaze passed over the shifting crowd, a familiar figure caught her eye. Despite everything, she found herself breaking into a smile. *This might be my favourite of all of Jackson's disguises so far!* Her megastar boyfriend could never go out in public as himself without attracting hordes of adoring fans.

This time he'd hidden his blond hair underneath a dull brown wig and he'd put on a pair of huge glasses that made him look adorably nerdy.

Aww. Olivia couldn't help giving a little bounce in her seat as she waved to him. *I have the cutest boyfriend ever!*

Her excitement vanished as the reality of the situation swept back over her . . . *at least for now.*

Jackson's smile was unmistakable, even through the disguise, but it slipped as he sat down beside her. Olivia felt her stomach sink as she took in his suddenly grave expression. *Oh no. Here come the questions!*

'Where are your parents?' he asked. 'Right before I went to my hotel to change they said they'd be meeting us here.'

Whew. At least that was an easy one to answer! 'They got sidetracked.' She grinned as she pointed to the movie theatre entrance that stood opposite the food court. 'Dad spotted this old kung-fu

57

movie he said Mom *had* to see and he dragged her off before she could say no. I guess it's a rerelease or something?' She shrugged. 'If you ask me, though, *Snake in the Eagle's Shadow* sounds more like a nature documentary.'

'Are you kidding me?' Jackson spun around to peer at the posters by the movie theatre entrance. 'That's a classic – and look, it's not starting for another five minutes. We've still got time. We should go, too!'

'Now you're the one who's kidding!' Olivia laughed in disbelief as her sophisticated Hollywood boyfriend suddenly turned into an excited little boy in front of her eyes. 'Jackson, there is no way I'm sitting through a kung-fu movie that's more than twice as old as I am, classic or not.'

'C'mon, Olivia!' Jackson grabbed her hand, tugging her up out of her seat. 'I promise, it won't feel dated. It was really ahead of its time! Let's just –'

'Jackson!' Olivia shook her head at him, laughing as she dug in her heels. Under normal circumstances she would have been more than happy to give in to his excitement, but this time she had a pre-trial to get through. 'Slow down, OK? I'm starving, and I haven't seen you for days. Can't we please just have a nice meal and watch a movie later?'

'Well . . . OK.' Jackson's famous megawatt grin shredded his dowdy disguise as he wrapped one arm around her shoulder. 'But I'm warning you: I'm booking you in for a DVD binge-watch of *all* my kung-fu favourites in exchange!'

'I'll even try to stay awake for all of them,' Olivia promised him. 'For your sake!'

Tipping her head against his shoulder, she walked with him towards the Italian family restaurant that stood just outside the main body of the mall.

'Please promise me you won't send Ivy in your

place when we have our movie marathon,' Jackson told her as they walked through the restaurant doors and the hostess waved them towards the closest empty table. 'There's no way my poor DVDs could withstand one of her death-squints!'

'I promise.' Olivia winced. 'I really am sorry about lunch today. I promise I wouldn't have swapped on you if it hadn't been important.'

'That's OK.' Jackson smiled as he pulled out a chair for her. 'I'm just glad to be here with you now.'

Olivia smiled at him, even though her stomach was doing backflips.

I hate trying to trick my own boyfriend!

'Well?' A high-pitched voice spoke directly behind her ears and a moment later a tall dark-haired waitress slammed two glasses of water on to the table so hard that they spilled. 'Are you two ready to order yet?'

'Huh?' Jerked out of her reverie, Olivia blinked

up at the waitress, whose long dark hair covered her face. 'We only just got here . . . and we haven't even gotten our menus yet.'

'Pfft.' The waitress grabbed two menus from the closest table, tossed them down in front of Olivia and stalked off.

'Wow.' Jackson gave a half-laugh. 'I guess she's having a bad night.'

'I guess so.' Olivia couldn't bring herself to worry about the waitress's rudeness, though. *It's time to get started.* Taking a deep breath, she picked up her menu and turned it around in her hands, over and over again. When Jackson didn't notice, she tapped her fingers on the table, still fiddling with the menu.

Finally, when the tips of her fingers were starting to hurt, her boyfriend looked up. 'You OK?' he asked, pulling his glasses down to peer at her over the top.

She called on all of her acting skills to give a

rueful smile and look her boyfriend directly in the eyes as she began his test. 'Can you teach me Russian?' she asked.

Jackson gave her a look like she'd just asked him that question *in* Russian.

'I mean, a Russian accent.'

Jackson cocked his head, confused. 'When would you need to do a Russian accent?'

Oh, stake me – I've already cornered myself. Here I am, trying to test Jackson's honesty, and I have to lie to do it!

'Oh, uhm, for school. Yeah, the Drama department is doing a showcase at the end of the semester, and I've been asked to play the part of a Russian . . . spy.'

Oh my gosh, that would be awesome, she thought. Then: *it's make-believe, Abbott, don't get excited.*

Jackson was grinning at her. 'Oh cool. And you're worried about the accent?'

'I can't do Russian,' Olivia said, pleased that at least that wasn't a lie. 'And I don't know anyone who can give me any coaching. Oh! What about Keith? His Russian accent in that movie last year was *soooo* good. Could he give me lessons over Skype, maybe?'

But Jackson only smiled and shook his head. 'If I know Keith, he'd be a horrible teacher. No way would he have the discipline for it. It'd drive you both crazy.'

Olivia had to move her hands under the table so that Jackson couldn't see her pump both fists. He had fed him the opportunity to sell out his friend, and he hadn't taken it.

But then she remembered what Ms Deborg said. She had to try *everything* to get him to break Keith's confidence. Asking once was hardly 'everything'.

'Please?' she said, leaning forwards. She thought about batting her eyelids at him, but that would be the *surest* way to signal to him that something was up. Olivia *never* batted her eyelids.

'You know me, I'm a perfectionist,' she went

on. 'I really, really want to do well. You don't think Keith could give me just a little help?'

Jackson didn't miss a beat. 'Keith won't be able to help you. He's . . . not cut out for coaching. Trust me on this.'

Olivia had to bite her cheeks to keep from smiling. Her boyfriend was – technically – lying to her, but that was OK! He was proving himself trustworthy.

But she knew she still hadn't tried *everything*.

'It doesn't matter,' she said, making a sort of sad face. 'My dancing will be worse than my accent.'

'What are you talking about? Why would a spy need to dance?'

Oh, garlic sandwiches! More lying to do. 'Oh, she, uh . . . goes undercover as a ballerina!'

'Sounds awesome.' Jackson grinned – the same grin she'd seen on so many posters and magazine covers. She used to smile when she saw it – now she just cringed.

'Yeah, yeah,' she mumbled. 'Totally awesome.'

'You won't have to worry about that. I've danced with you before, remember? I know you're good!'

Aww. Olivia's cheeks heated in a blush as she looked down at the menu to hide her expression. Still, she couldn't let it go that easily. 'OK, I'm not terrible,' she said, 'but I'm not great, either. So . . .' She slid him a glance. 'It was definitely silly of me to say yes to playing a ballerina! Don't you think? But it's a live performance, so it's not like I could get a body double, or anything like that.'

Holding her breath, she met his gaze full-on. *Is he going to say anything?*

She'd given him the perfect set-up to share the juicy gossip about Keith . . . but his blue eyes were clear and guileless.

'I think you'd be great as a ballerina spy,' Jackson said. 'But then, I'm pretty sure you'd be great at anything you really wanted to do. You work too hard *not* to be.' He looked down at his menu. 'What do you think? Should we order starters?'

Whew. Olivia didn't realise how tense she was until she felt her fists unclench. *He did it! He kept Keith's secret . . . and passed the second pre-trial!*

Before she could answer, the long-haired waitress suddenly appeared as if out of nowhere, holding out a plate of fried cheese-balls . . . but this time her hair had been tied back.

Olivia sucked in a breath. *Ms Deborg!*

The vampire secretary didn't even spare Olivia a glance as she slid the plate on to the table. 'On the house!' she chirped to Jackson. 'I'm such a big fan of your movies.'

Jackson choked on his water and started to cough. 'H-H-How . . . How did you recognise me?' he finally managed.

'How could I not?' Ms Deborg gave a shriek-laugh as she waved one hand. 'My daughters are so obsessed by you – your face is all over the walls of our apartment. I'd recognise you anywhere!'

Yikes! Who thought Ms Deborg would be that good of an actor herself?! Olivia marvelled, a little scared at the secretary's complete change in demeanour.

Jackson smiled conspiratorially as he leaned towards the disguised vampire. 'Listen,' he murmured. 'I would really appreciate if you could not tell anyone else, OK? I'll sign anything you'd like for your daughters, but . . .' He shrugged and gave her a rueful laugh. 'I'm sure you can appreciate the need for a little discretion.'

Ha! Olivia had to look away from the disgruntled look on Ms Deborg's face to keep herself from laughing out loud.

If only Jackson knew who he was talking to!

But she'd never been so proud of her megastar boyfriend . . . because without even knowing it he'd just shown the Vampire Round Table that he understood *exactly* how important it was to be discreet and keep a secret.

As the 'waitress' flounced away, Olivia's

shoulders relaxed for the first time in ages.

'What's up?' Jackson said. 'You look excited.'

'I'm just happy to be here with you,' she said.

But silently, she added: *and I just might be able to stay with you forever after all!*

Chapter Four

I vy fidgeted in her seat the next night, sneaking glances at the tall grandfather clock that stood in the Vegas' dining room. Her dad and stepmom sat across from her at the dinner table, where – in just a little while – the two of them would be conducting Jackson's third and final pre-trial. It was already set with their best china, even though their food had only just begun cooking in the oven. The tension in the air was so thick that it made Ivy's skin itch.

Within a half an hour, they would all know for certain whether Jackson was going to be allowed to undergo the *real* Three Tests . . .

This is awful! Ivy couldn't sit in one place any longer. She shoved her chair back from the table and started pacing. 'I don't even understand the point of this last pre-trial. Olivia already tested Jackson's honesty last night, didn't she? Why do you need to test it again tonight?'

Charles just nodded. 'Olivia tested Jackson's ability to keep a secret,' he said. 'Tonight, I will be asking him questions to determine the strength of his word. That's a different issue.'

Ivy shook her head as she spun on her heel to pace back the way she had come. 'How will you even tell if he's lying, though?'

When she saw her dad and stepmom share a look, Ivy stopped pacing again. 'What? What is it?'

Charles nodded at Lillian, as if to say it was OK to tell Ivy . . . something.

Lillian looked to Ivy. 'Vampires have ways of . . . *hearing* dishonesty,' she said gently.

Wait a minute, we do? Ivy thought about how easily

70

she'd been catching people out in lies just lately. She had been beginning to think she was just super-smart, or that she could really, really *read* people.

But maybe it was just another vampire thing – like the super-hearing, the speed and agility.

'So . . .' She frowned and looked at Lillian. 'Will you hear Jackson's pulse if he tells a lie? Like, hear it make a thrumming sound . . . something like that?'

Lillian traded a startled glance with Charles. 'Ivy, what are you talking about?'

'It's just . . . what you just said,' Ivy mumbled. 'I think that's been happening to me.'

Charles crossed the dining room, coming to stand in front of Ivy. 'Tell us exactly what's been going on.'

'Well, lately,' she said, 'I seem to be able to tell if someone's not telling the truth. It's like a thrumming sound in my mind. Is . . . that normal? Well, is it *vampire* normal?'

Charles and Lillian traded a long look.

'OK, you have to start talking to me right now!' Ivy burst out. 'This is starting to freak me out, and you're not helping. What's wrong with me?'

'There's nothing wrong with you,' her father said firmly. 'But it's possible that you are developing your ninth sense . . . rather unexpectedly early.'

'*Ninth?*' Ivy let out a startled half-laugh. 'Don't you mean sixth?'

'No.' Charles shook his head decisively. 'Human senses may be limited to five, but vampires have far more. The sixth sense allows us to feel the presence of others, the seventh gives us the ability to detect when it is going to rain, the eighth sense allows us to detect when someone is sick, and the ninth . . .' His shoulders rose and fell with his breath. 'The ninth is the ability to tell when someone is lying to you.'

'Whoa.' Ivy shook her head in wonder as she sat back down at the table. 'I never knew about any of those.'

'Not every vampire develops each sense perfectly,' Lillian told her. 'Some of the extra four are more powerful than others . . . and all of them are expected to develop when a vampire is an adult, *not* a teenager.'

Charles was smiling at her. 'As soon as all this business with Jackson is over, I insist that you call your grandparents in Transylvania to give them the good news yourself. My parents will be thrilled . . .' His lips curved into an outright smirk. 'And my sisters will be *very* jealous, because not one of their children has had this happen. I only wish I could be there to *see* their reactions!'

Lillian rolled her eyes. 'This isn't a contest, dear.'

Charles raised his hands. 'I am only excited because *this* is all so exciting. Tell me you're not thrilled that our Ivy is so special?'

Lillian seemed like she was trying to be serious – until she, too, smiled. 'It is fantastic. Ivy, you've developed the ninth sense, and you're only fourteen. No one will ever be able to lie to you ever again!'

Ivy was about to scoff and ask what good that could do, when she realised that being a living, breathing lie-detector was kind of a handy skill for an investigative reporter.

The doorbell rang and Ivy was startled out of her thoughts.

'I'll explain everything later,' Charles told her. 'But remember: for now we must be silent on the subject!'

'I know, I know,' she called back as she sped out into the front hallway. *Icks-nay on the ampire-vay uff-stay when Jackson's around!* She rolled her eyes. Did he really think she would forget after all this time?

But, hey . . . She drew to a halt for a moment, smiling at the sudden realisation: *tomorrow, that rule might no longer apply!* If tonight went well . . .

She flung the door open . . . then winced.

Uh-oh. She'd been so busy worrying about her

ninth sense she'd completely forgotten to come up with a good way of separating Jackson from Olivia for the last pre-trial!

'Um . . .' She closed her eyes briefly, trying to think fast as she ushered the two humans into the house. 'I'm really sorry, Jackson, but would if it be OK if I talk to Olivia alone in my room for just a couple of minutes? I'm . . . uh . . . really upset. About . . .' Her mind went blank. '. . . Something?'

Oh yeah, real smooth, Ivy. Sooooo convincing.

Jackson's eyebrows shot up. 'Of course.' He hung his coat on the hook and stepped back. 'I'll wait for you guys in the dining room. But Ivy . . .' He gave her a look of deep concern. 'Whatever's going on with Brendan . . . I'm sure it'll be OK. You guys are really great together.'

'Thanks.' Ivy restrained herself from rolling her eyes as she tugged Olivia with her towards the stairs.

Why did boys always assume that *boys* were the only things that girls ever got upset about?

Still, her ruse had worked. As Jackson headed towards the dining room, Ivy and Olivia hurried upstairs to Ivy's room, where Ivy's old bed had been turned into a specially made half-coffin, half-bed bunkbed for when Olivia slept over.

'Oof.' Olivia flopped down in the coffin bunk, her face pale. 'I hate that we can't be down there with them. Do you think it'll go well?'

Ivy wanted to reassure her sister, but she felt the same tension in her own stomach. Silently, she gave Olivia's shoulder a soft squeeze . . .

. . . Because even if Jackson did pass Charles's lie detector test she knew that much, much worse was coming for him.

He might have loved Olivia very much, but that alone did not mean that he would be able to pass the Three Tests.

🦇 🦇 🦇

Olivia shifted in Ivy's coffin, trying to get comfortable. If she didn't hear anything from downstairs soon, she was going to explode! She'd been waiting with Ivy for what felt like hours. Normally she loved hanging out with her twin, but tonight she felt so wound up with worry about her boyfriend that she had to force herself to concentrate on what Ivy was saying, about her strange new talent.

'. . . so I can just *tell* when someone's telling a lie. Dad and Lillian think it's a really cool thing and that they'll explain after all this with Jackson is settled. But, yeah . . . vamps get extra senses, and I'm getting my first one.'

Olivia focused on the relevant part. 'So, if Dad's questioning Jackson to test his honesty . . . Dad must have that ninth sense, too? You inherited it from him, maybe?'

Ivy nodded. 'I guess so.'

'Of course.' Olivia gave a half-laugh as she sat up. 'Do you ever get the feeling that you inherited all the Good Stuff from our twinness?'

'Trust me . . .' Ivy rubbed one of her eyes, grimacing. 'You wouldn't say that if you were the one who had to wear coloured contacts every day! Did I ever tell you . . .'

But no matter how much she tried, Olivia just couldn't focus on Ivy's words. She knew her sister was trying to keep her distracted, but every inch of her body was attuned to the tiny creaks of wood and faint hum of voices coming up through the bedroom floorboards from the kitchen below. The whole future of her relationship was being decided down there without her! *How am I supposed to think about anything else?*

Her fingers tightened more and more and around the sides of Ivy's coffin bed as she listened with all her might, just waiting to hear the sound of slamming doors or her boyfriend's voice rising in anger. If Jackson stormed out in outrage at the interrogation he was being put through, then the pre-trial would be over . . . and she would never be allowed to share the truth about her family with him.

But the next sound she heard was her stepmom's voice, rising from the bottom of the stairs. 'Hey, you two!' Lillian called with mock-indignation. 'I hope you don't think you can get out of helping with dinner by hiding up there!'

'Whew!' Ivy sprang to her feet with vamp agility and headed for the door. 'That's our signal!'

Olivia had been waiting for so long for this verdict! *Please, please, please let him have passed* . . .

As she stepped into the kitchen, Olivia looked straight past her boyfriend, who sat at the breakfast bar picking at a bowl of pretzels, to her bio-dad, who stood by the fridge.

Please, please, please . . .

Charles smiled and gave her a tiny, approving nod.

Thank goodness! Relief flooded through her in such an overpowering wave that Olivia had to grab the kitchen door frame to keep her balance. Jackson had passed all three of his preliminary trials! But as quickly as the relief flooded her it was kicked aside by a tingle of dread in her belly – this was just the beginning.

Now, Jackson would be told the truth.

Charles cleared his throat. 'I think Olivia and Jackson ought to be left alone for a few minutes.'

Jackson looked up from the pretzels, his eyebrows flying upward. 'Um . . . OK?'

'What?' Olivia stared at her dad. 'But . . .' *Aren't you going to be here while I tell him?*

She knew that the responsibility was hers, but she might need her twin, her bio-dad and stepmom – *actual* vamps – to back her up and convince Jackson that she was not making any of this up.

'This is between the two of you,' said Charles, with a meaningful look.

Olivia swallowed hard. Then she nodded. 'You're right,' she said. This might have been a vampire secret, but it was Olivia who had set it all in motion. Telling Jackson was her responsibility.

Lillian only gave her a sympathetic smile as she walked past. Charles gave her a firm nod on his way out, but her twin stopped to give her a hug. 'You can do this,' Ivy said softly.

Then she closed the door behind her, leaving Olivia and her boyfriend alone in the kitchen.

Olivia turned to see Jackson still sitting at the breakfast bar. He had pushed the bowl of pretzels aside, his fists clenched with nerves – his knuckles were ghost-white. 'OK . . . now I'm getting really worried.' Jackson gave Olivia a bemused look as she straightened. 'Are you dumping me, or something?'

'No!' Olivia said. 'I just . . . umm . . .' She walked over and sank down on to the tall stool beside him, her mind whirling. How could she possibly explain the truth about her family – about the secret Franklin Grove community?

'Come on, Olivia,' Jackson said. 'What's going

on? Everyone in this house has been acting really weird tonight. You should have heard the questions Mr Vega was asking me. "What would you do if you found a bag full of money on the street?" "Do you like getting so much fanmail?" It was like he was interviewing me for a job or something!'

'Um.' Olivia smiled weakly. 'Not quite.' She met her boyfriend's clear blue gaze and forced herself to not look away. 'But I did promise you that I'd explain all that strangeness that happened over Halloween.'

Jackson popped another pretzel in his mouth, but didn't look away from her. 'Yeah, you did. And I'm really glad you're bringing it up cos –'

'Hang on, let me say this . . .' She took another deep breath, then squeezed her eyes shut and let it all out in a rapid burst: 'So, here's the thing: vampires are real, and they're spread all over the world, but they're definitely not scary . . . and they're my family! Charles and Lillian are both vamps, and so is Ivy. There's a whole vamp community in Franklin Grove!'

She had to stop to gulp a breath, but she kept her eyes tightly closed so she wouldn't have to look her boyfriend in the face. 'You know how everyone thinks that Mr Vega is Ivy's adoptive dad? Well, he's not her adoptive dad. He's her real dad ... and he's my bio-dad, too. But our mom was human – that's why I'm human, but it's super-complicated and I don't really understand it if I'm honest – and Ivy and I were separated after our mom died. Dad thought it would be better for me to be brought up with other humans, so he gave me up for adoption when I was still a baby. It was just weird good luck that brought us all back together again here in Franklin Grove ... but since I'm a human, I had to undergo Three Tests to prove that I could be trusted to keep the vampire secret. The whole community is so secretive they won't let anyone find out the truth without putting them through the Tests, and . . . now it's your turn.'

Her lips shuddered as she let out a shaky breath. Then she started laughing, because – well, it was kind of ridiculous when she put it into a speech like that! She almost didn't expect Jackson to still be there when she opened her eyes.

'I mean . . . if you want to,' she said. 'It's totally your choice, but . . . I just don't want to keep any secrets from you any more. So, there it is . . . Now you know everything.'

Whew. Finally, she opened her eyes . . .

. . . and found Jackson staring at her with his mouth hanging open and a half-eaten pretzel still visible on his tongue.

Whoa. Olivia blinked. It was the first time she'd ever seen her megastar boyfriend looking so *un*-Hollywood-smooth! *I guess I really did surprise him this time.*

As she watched, he shook his head, then finally swallowed the rest of his pretzel with a gulp.

84

'Wow,' he said. 'I mean, *wow*. You've played some really weird pranks on me before, Olivia, but this has got to be the strangest one yet.' He laughed as he shook his head again, even more vigorously, as if he were shaking her words out of his memory. 'You know, if you really don't want to tell me what was behind all that Halloween stuff, you could just *say* that it's a secret. You don't have to make up some crazy story to explain it!'

'I'm not making any of this up!' Olivia grabbed his hands. 'I'm not playing a prank on you. I'm serious, Jackson.'

He smiled at her, reaching out to stroke her hair. 'I love you, Olivia, but you really do have the weirdest sense of humour sometimes. Remember that time you pranked me by taking me to a graveyard, for no reason at all?'

'The reason I took you to that graveyard was because, back then, I thought *you* might be a vamp. So I thought you'd like the atmosphere!'

'The – *what?* Never mind.' Jackson scooted his chair back. 'You know what, this joke would have worked a lot better on Halloween. Why don't we just forget it and move on now, OK?'

'Ohh . . .!' Olivia ran her hands through her hair, feeling totally stressed out. All that time spent working up to telling him the big secret and he didn't believe her.

How ridiculous is my life right now? she wondered. *I'm trying to convince my movie-star boyfriend that vamps are real, and that some of them are my family. Someone should make a movie about* this . . .

'Look.' She jumped off the bar stool. 'I *will* prove this to you. Just wait here, please – don't run away because you think your girlfriend's gone a bit crazy!'

She hurried out of the room, finding the rest of her vamp family sitting in the living room, looking at least as tense as she felt. With their super-hearing, she didn't need to tell them how it had been going. 'What am I going to do?' she asked. 'I don't know how to prove to him that I'm not joking.'

'Let me come in with you,' Ivy said. Her kohl-lined eyes narrowed as she marched over to join Olivia. 'If we both tell him the same thing, maybe he'll finally get the message!'

They walked together back into the kitchen, where Jackson was frowning down at an uneaten pretzel in his hand. He sighed when he saw Ivy by Olivia's side.

'Oh no. She hasn't dragged you into this prank too, has she?'

'It's all true,' Ivy said flatly. 'She's not teasing you, Jackson.'

'Oh, come on . . .!' He popped the pretzel into his mouth. 'I told you – this might have worked for Halloween, but we're way past that now. I don't know what you're trying to do. But, Ivy, I've been out with you in broad daylight, so I know that you can handle it. And, if you're a vampire, where are your fangs, huh?'

Aha! 'That's it,' Olivia said. 'Jackson needs to *see* it to believe it.' She smiled. 'Ivy, take out your eyes!'

'*What?*' Jackson stared at them.

Ivy grinned back at Olivia. 'That is a *fangtastic* idea.' Tipping her head forwards, she raised her fingers to her eyes.

'Oh, you mean *contact* lenses.' Jackson rolled his eyes, relaxing back on his seat. 'And what exactly is that supposed to prove?'

'Just wait and see.' Olivia crossed over to stand by Jackson's bar stool as her sister turned away from them and crossed to the opposite kitchen counter. Still facing away from them, Ivy took the lenses from her eyes and carefully placed them on the side. Then she stood still for a moment, her black hair falling across her face as she kept

88

her head tipped down, building the anticipation.

Olivia smiled ruefully as she felt Jackson growing more and more tense in the seat beside her. *I may be the actress in this family, but my twin certainly does have a flair for drama!*

Finally, Ivy turned around . . . but her eyes were tightly closed.

Olivia slipped her hand into her boyfriend's. 'Brace yourself,' she whispered. 'And whatever you feel, please don't run, OK?'

'Of course I'm not going to – aahhhh!' Jackson leaped to his feet, almost dragging Olivia to the ground as Ivy opened her eyes, revealing vivid inhuman purple irises.

The Violet Truth! Olivia thought wryly, as she felt him squeezing her hand.

No one could see Ivy's natural eyes and think that she was an ordinary human.

Jackson opened his mouth as if to speak, but no

coherent words came out. 'Uh – uhm . . . *erm* . . .'

Uh-oh. I think my boyfriend's forgotten the English language!

'It's OK,' Olivia said soothingly. She nudged gently on his shoulders until he sank back down on to his bar stool, still staring at her twin. 'I was shocked the first time I saw her eyes, too.'

'They are shocking,' Ivy said smugly. She leaned back against the counter, crossing her arms. 'Shockingly awesome, huh? And, just so there's no confusion . . . Oh, you two ought to stand back a little bit.'

Olivia had to pull Jackson back from the breakfast bar – he was so stunned he could barely move.

Ivy stepped forwards into a perfect handstand.

Jackson gave a nervous laugh. 'So? It's a handstand. Olivia used to be a cheerleader, so of course you have the same –'

Then Ivy pushed herself up so that she was balancing on the tips of her fingers.

'Whoa!' Jackson gasped, looking from Ivy to Olivia and back again. 'That's . . . That's . . .'

Olivia winked at her sister. 'Pretty impressive, huh?'

'Wow.' Jackson swallowed visibly and shook his head, slumping back down on to a stool at the breakfast bar. 'Wow.' He stared at the wall, then gave a gentle laugh. 'Well. I guess a lot of things suddenly make sense about Franklin Grove.'

Olivia sat down on the stool next to him and wrapped her arms around him. 'Are you OK?' She could feel his heart thudding hard against her arm as she hugged him close. 'You don't have to be scared. Vamps aren't really scary. They don't attack humans, or –'

'I'm not scared.' Jackson hugged her back, then gently set her aside, looking past her to Ivy. 'I know you guys, remember? If *Ivy*'s a vamp, then vamps must be OK. It's just . . . going to take me a little while to deal with the shock of it. I never even imagined anything like this could ever be real.'

'Of course.' Olivia nibbled on her lower lip, sliding him a worried look. 'And . . . are you mad at me for not telling you before?'

Jackson frowned thoughtfully, his gaze turning inward for a moment. 'Y'know . . . I'm really not.' He gave her a wry grin. 'It was hard enough for me to believe it tonight. If you'd told me before we'd known each other for so long . . . I might have felt differently. But anyway, it's not the kind of thing you can just blurt out to someone, is it?'

'Nope.' But Olivia didn't stop fidgeting. 'The thing is . . . you have to understand what's coming next. Remember how I told you about the Three Tests? The Vampire Round Table is going to test you, too . . . and they are *serious* about the consequences. If you fail, they'll actually alter your memory.'

'They can do that?' Jackson sounded fascinated.

Ivy finally dropped back to her feet, her violet

eyes narrowed grimly. 'Better believe it,' she said. 'And if you fail, they won't just make you forget that vampires are real – they'll make you forget that you and Olivia were ever an item. In fact, they'll make you think you disliked her.'

'Well, then.' Jackson flashed his famous Hollywood grin at them both. 'It's a good thing I won't fail! Bring on the Tests.'

Warmth filled Olivia's chest as she met his gaze and read the open affection there. It was wonderful to have a boyfriend who loved her so much that he would undergo the Tests without hesitation . . . but she, of all people, knew just how hard and frightening those Tests could be.

Whatever it takes, she thought to herself, *we will make sure that Jackson is ready for what's next.*

Chapter Five

When the creaky old school bus shuddered to a halt in front of Franklin Grove High School the next morning, Ivy didn't even wait for Olivia and Brendan to finish gathering up their bags. She just lunged for the door, her big black boots clattering down against the metal aisle.

As she leaped outside, she sucked in a deep lungful of fresh air . . . and the wonderful feeling of freedom.

Finally, I'm out of that bus full of phonies*!*

Her dad might call her new, ninth sense 'a gift', but to Ivy it was starting to feel more like a curse. All around her in the crowded bus, the sound of people's lies had battered against her senses like tiny little hammers: athletes lying about just how fast they could run; honour students lying to their friends about how *unbelievably easy* they'd found their last history test; one girl had even lied about how much her new clothes had cost!

Can't anyone just tell the truth any more? Ivy braced herself as she joined the central stream of students heading into the main school entrance. *I'm not sure how much more of this I can stand before I have to death-squint this whole place into oblivion!*

'Hey you!' Her best friend, Sophia, bumped Ivy's shoulder gently as she fell into step beside her on the way through the big front doors. Sophia looked as stylish as ever in a slim-fitting black wrap-dress under a wool coat and wedge-heeled black ankle-boots. She raised one eyebrow as she and Ivy walked towards their neighbouring lockers. 'Someone woke up on the wrong side of the coffin today. Why are you looking so grim?'

'Because this school is filled with a big bunch of lying liary liars,' Ivy growled as she banged her locker door open and threw her coat inside.

'Oh come on.' Sophia shrugged off her own coat and shook her head. 'I know you've got your brand new sense, but that doesn't mean *everybody's* lying all the time.'

'That's not what it feels like . . .' Ivy began. Then she stopped, as a familiar figure strode up to them.

'Aha, Sophia!' It was Amelia Thomson, the senior Queen of the Goths. She smirked as she wagged a finger at them. 'I hear *someone* has a bit of a crush!'

As Ivy watched in shock, her cool, collected, fashionista best friend suddenly turned deathly pale – which was the vampire's equivalent of a raging blush – and tried to hide behind her locker door.

'Seriously?' Ivy demanded. She shook her head in disbelief as she stared at Sophia's pale face.

'You have a crush on someone and Amelia knew before I did?'

'Um . . .' Sophia looked deeply pained, but didn't say a single word.

Of course, Ivy realised. Sophia wasn't going to speak . . . because she knew she couldn't lie to Ivy now!

'So much for best friendship,' Ivy muttered. 'I can't believe you didn't tell me!'

Amelia snickered. 'Are you sure about that best friendship?' she asked playfully. 'Surely a *real* best friend would have noticed the way Sophia's been mooning after AJ for at least a week.'

'*AJ?*' Ivy repeated. She looked from Amelia to Sophia, torn between feeling offended and excited for her friend. 'AJ-from-Music-Theory-AJ? *Really?*'

'Ahh!' Sophia slammed her locker door shut. 'Forget it,' she said. 'I don't want to talk about it with either one of you!' Chin held high, she stalked away, leaving Ivy staring after her.

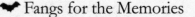

'Tsk.' Smiling, Amelia moved on. 'See you later, Ivy.'

Ivy couldn't even bring herself to say goodbye. As she turned back to her locker, depression weighted down her shoulders. *Even my own best friend has been hiding the truth from me!*

As the hall behind her filled with chatting, gossiping groups, her truth-sense hammered at her again and again, pointing out every single exaggeration or outright lie, until she had to restrain herself from banging her head against her locker door. *This ninth sense really isn't all I'd cracked it up to be!*

It was as if the whole world had become one gigantic subtitled movie . . . and she couldn't stop reading the nasty truths scrolling underneath the glossy-looking images.

Gritting her teeth, she reached into her black backpack, pulling out all the textbooks that she didn't need for her first few classes and dumping them in her locker as loudly as she could. Still, she couldn't shut out the sound of a tenth-grader behind her, Eva Brennan, one of the bunny girls, talking to one of her friends as they passed.

'I'm *so* sorry to have to cancel Friday's sleepover, Fleur! But Mom and Dad had a really big fight, so the whole house is tense, and, weeelllll . . .'

Eva is totally lying.

But why would anyone lie about their parents fighting?

Ivy could not help the huff of disbelief as she closed her locker door shut. Eva stopped and looked back at her. 'Did you say something?'

Ivy stared back at her. *No, I didn't,* she thought. *But I* could *say that you're a big liar . . . although I don't know what you're lying about.*

Instead of saying that, though, Ivy just shook her head. After peering at Ivy for a second longer, Eva moved on.

Ivy shook her head. *I'd make a killer gossip*

columnist – if only I didn't hate gossip so very much!

She started down the corridor towards the music wing. Lately, Music Theory hadn't exactly been the most thrilling of classes, but today, there was a noticeable buzz of excitement in the air as she walked towards the classroom. She frowned as she took in all the whispering groups around her . . . then remembered.

Oh, yeah. It's the new teacher's first day!

Their first teacher, Ms Noonan, had quit the school in a blaze of glory two weeks earlier, when she'd suddenly jumped up from her desk in the middle of class and declared that she was 'giving up the humdrum, ordinary life of a loser to start a band and find my destiny!'

She'd even left an ear-splittingly terrible song on the principal's voicemail to announce her resignation . . . which he'd managed to play over the PA system to the whole school by mistake. Ms Noonan had hardly been a great teacher, but the substitutes who'd filled in for her hadn't known anything about music theory, so class had turned into a mind-numbingly boring series of 'watch old music videos and talk about them' snore-fests.

As she neared the open doorway, she heard more and more whispers circling through the hall.

'Mr Hawkins told me he was a guitarist in a major rock band before he came here . . .'

'. . . *and* an award-winning songwriter, too!'

Hmph. Ivy snorted. *I don't need to be a walking lie-detector to know that's not the whole truth!*

Award-winning songwriters generally made a lot of money, didn't they? *Somehow I can't imagine a real rock star coming to teach at Franklin Grove High School!*

As Ivy stepped into the room her eyes went straight to Sophia, who sat looking tense at her usual desk in the third row. *Is she still mad?* Ivy glanced at the empty desk beside her best friend . . . and was relieved to see that Sophia had set down her faux-leather satchel to save the seat for

Ivy. As Ivy slid into place, she finally glanced at the new teacher.

'Huh.' She wasn't sure *what* she'd been expecting, but it was not the frizzy brown-grey ponytail that trailed down Mr Hawkins's back, nor was it the too-tight black T-shirt with a flaming bull's skull on it. And it definitely wasn't the intricate tattoos that covered both forearms. 'Whoa. I don't think I've ever seen a teacher with tattoos before,' she said. 'He's certainly trying to look the part, anyway.'

'So you've heard the rumours, too?' Sophia cocked her head meaningfully. 'Do you think he really was a rock star before this?'

Ivy shrugged. 'I don't know of too many real rock stars who gave up their careers to teach high school. Even if his band folded, wouldn't he have retired to some fancy estate out in Malibu?'

'Not if he'd squandered his money.' Sophia narrowed her eyes as she studied their teacher, who was looking ecstatic as he swept his arms wide in an imaginary flip of his air guitar. '*I've* heard that a lot of musicians blow their bank accounts on all sorts of crazy stuff, like yachts and motorbikes. Or maybe a greedy record company gave him a bad deal. Maybe they stole all the money from his hit songs. Come on, Ivy Vega!' Sophia reached over and gave her a playful nudge. 'You don't have to think the worst of people every single time!'

'Oh yeah?' Ivy shoved her back, grinning. 'You know I don't. For instance . . .' She tipped her head towards AJ Tripathi, who sat at the front of the room, bent over a music magazine.

'Oh . . . well . . .' Sophia blinked, then looked away quickly.

Gotcha. Ivy smirked.

Amelia was right: Sophia was *so* crushing on AJ!

'Ahem!' Mr Hawkins started playing air guitar as he jumped to his feet. 'It's time to get this concert started!' he declared.

'It's not a concert,' mumbled Fleur Evans, one of the bunny girls. 'It's class.'

'Wrong, young lady.' Mr Hawkins never stopped air-strumming. 'All of life is a concert, and I should know – I've played in hundreds of them.'

A murmur of interest went through the crowd, students firing questions – where were the concerts? What was his favourite show? Did he play with anyone famous?

Mr Hawkins just held up his hands, just as Ivy's boyfriend hurried through the door. 'Silence, everybody!' called the teacher.

Brendan came to a halt, his eyebrows rising as an expectant silence fell over the room. He glanced wide-eyed at Ivy, then – with another look at their teacher – grabbed the desk closest to the door as if he didn't dare cross the room to his usual place.

Ivy didn't blame him. From the look on their teacher's face, he might be about to break into song at any moment.

I hope at least it's better than Ms Noonan's goodbye song . . .

The whole class waited . . .

And kept on waiting.

Seconds turned into minutes. Mr Hawkins remained as still as a statue.

Someone coughed.

Feet shuffled.

Sophia gave Ivy a confused glance as the silence built and built around them.

Ivy gave the subtlest shrug she could pull off, hoping that Mr Hawkins wouldn't notice the tiny rustling sound that her cotton sweater made. *I have no idea what's going on either!*

Finally someone broke the spell. Fleur flung her hand up even as she spoke. 'Uh, Mr Hawkins, are you OK? Shouldn't you be, like, teaching us now?'

'I'm trying to teach you.' Mr Hawkins spun around, grinning.

Fleur made a face. 'Teach us *what*?'

Mr Hawkins sang in a whisper-quiet but surprisingly melodic voice: *'You should not mistake lack of noise for siiiiiilence!'*

Um . . .? Ivy's eyebrows shot up as students all around the room shook their heads and traded baffled looks. Their new teacher might as well have been speaking in a foreign language for all the sense that he made, but at least now she knew one thing for sure: whether he was an ex-rock musician or not, he was a really good singer.

The next moment Mr Hawkins dropped back into a normal speaking voice as he perched on one corner of his desk, waving his hands emphatically and speaking so quickly that Ivy had to focus hard to catch all of his words. *'No one* can become a musician until they fully understand the true meaning of music. What *is* music? Well . . .' He threw out his arms, looking across the room, but didn't wait for any of his confused students to answer. 'It is many things! *So* many! But every song, every concerto, every symphony ever written has one single thing in common: *silence.*'

Ohhh-kay . . . Ivy looked down at her desk, trying not to laugh.

All around her, the room was full of stunned faces. Even Fleur looked shocked – or confused – into speechlessness.

At least now he has all the silence that he could ask for!

But even though Mr Hawkins's ideas were seriously weird, Ivy's truth-radar hadn't pinged once as he spoke. Her new teacher might be crazy, but at least he wasn't lying. He was telling the truth exactly as he saw it.

Finally, Brendan bravely raised his hand. 'Um . . . I'm sorry, Mr Hawkins, but what are you talking about? Sir?'

'Ahhh.' Mr Hawkins broke back into song, louder this time. *'Mr Hawwwwkins, what are you tawwwwkin' 'bout . . .'* He beamed, lingering over the near-rhyme, then fell back into normal speech. 'You see silence is *constant*, underneath all the noise.'

Ivy couldn't help herself. She sniggered. 'That makes no sense.' As a nervous titter sounded behind her and the whole class turned to stare at her, she shook her head at their new teacher. 'Look, noise is the *breaking* of silence, OK? You can't have silence if there's music at the same time!'

'Oh no?' Half-dancing, half-walking, Mr Hawkins grooved his way across the room towards her, clicking his fingers in time with his words. 'No silence if there's music? Is that what you really think? Is your mind really so thirsty? Is it starving for a drink?' Leaning over Ivy's desk, he shook his shoulders and clicked his fingers directly in her face. 'So just because it's night-time here in little Franklin Grove, you think it's night-time everywhere in the world, my *dove*?'

'No!' Grimacing, Ivy leaned as far back in her desk as she could manage. 'Of course not. That's totally different – for one thing, the Earth is rotating! And –'

'*You will understand soon . . .*' His singing voice rang out through the room like a deep bell as Mr Hawkins spun away from her. 'Soon, you will hear the silence as loudly as thunder.'

Aargh. Ivy ground her teeth as she straightened in her seat. *Now I wish we had our boring substitute teachers back for more videos!*

Mr Hawkins didn't spare her a single look as he strode back to the front of the class. 'The lesson of the day, my friends, is this: *silence is at the root of all sound.*'

That last line almost sounded like something Olivia's dad would say, Ivy thought ruefully. *Maybe I should introduce them . . . No, wait. Actually, I'd better not.*

Ivy shifted in her seat, trying to settle enough to concentrate on Mr Hawkins's ongoing monologue.

'. . . and before you can fully appreciate sound, you must first appreciate silence. So, for the final

forty minutes of this class, this is what we will do.'
He folded his hands together prayerfully in front
of his chest. 'We will attain . . . an appreciation . . .
of *silence.*'

'Are you *serious*?' Fleur demanded. 'You want us
to sit here and be quiet for the *whole class*?'

'Mmm.' Mr Hawkins smiled serenely. 'As soon
as your mouth closes, we will begin.'

Fleur gave an angry huff. 'This is supposed to
be a class about *music*, remember? And everyone's
been saying you were in a rock band. If that's true,
shouldn't you be all about noise?'

'Young lady . . .' Mr Hawkins raised one finger.
'Yes, I was in a rock band . . .'

Wait a minute. Ivy's head snapped up. *Was that a
quickening heartbeat I just heard?*

'. . . but this is not up for discussion,' Mr Hawkins
continued. 'Discussion breaks the precious silence
– and you cannot appreciate silence if it is broken.'

Grrr. Ivy had to stick her hands under her legs

to stop herself from throwing them up in the air. *He's just totally contradicting himself now!*

But she couldn't even call him on it, because the whole class had to sit in simmering silence until the bell rang . . . forty-one minutes later.

Finally! Scooping up her black backpack, Ivy leaped to her feet. Unfortunately, everyone else was in just as much of a hurry to escape, so she had to wait in the middle of the crowd to slowly file out of the room.

'I can't believe this!' Fleur raged ahead of her. 'This class totally sucks now. Mr Hawkins didn't even play a single song! This is supposed to be a *music* theory class, not a *silence* theory class.'

'Hmm . . .' Fleur's friend Eva looked like she had just woken up. 'You know, Fleur, I never realised before, but your voice is really, really . . . *loud.*'

Ha. Ivy suppressed a snicker as she shuffled forwards with the rest of the class. *You should hear it with vampire ears.*

'Of course it's loud,' Fleur snapped. 'I haven't used it in almost an hour. I can practically *feel* the silence tickling my ears!'

'It's so cool, isn't it?' Eva said wistfully as they stepped together through the door. 'I've never really thought about silence before.'

'Ha!' Fleur's furious voice hammered into Ivy's ears as they all moved into the hallway outside. 'Well, *I* think Mr Hawkins is a nutcase. Just because he was in a rock band, he thinks he knows everything!'

'He wasn't in a rock band,' Ivy muttered to Sophia.

'Huh?' Sophia peered at her as they came to a stop by their lockers. 'What are you talking about?'

'Hawkins,' said Ivy, keeping her voice low, 'he wasn't in a rock band. I don't know why he's –'

'What are you two whispering about?' Fleur appeared at Ivy's side, flanked by Eva and a few other girls.

Oops. Ivy winced. *This lie-detection sense is getting*

112

in the way of normal hearing! She shrugged, trading a helpless look with Sophia. 'I just . . . uh . . . think he might not have been in a rock band, that's all. I mean, what self-respecting rocker *likes* silence?'

'Hmm.' Fleur's eyes narrowed.

'Oh, look. There's Brendan!' Spotting her boyfriend waiting for her further down the hall, Ivy grabbed Sophia's shirtsleeve and hurried towards him, grateful to be out of that sticky situation

But when she glanced back a minute later, she saw Fleur still watching her with a dangerously thoughtful expression.

🦇   🦇   🦇

Olivia held Jackson's hand all through the elevator ride up to the second floor of Pentagon Court that afternoon after school. Her bio-dad stood behind them – a silent, supportive presence.

When the doors slid open Olivia made to step out, but Jackson didn't move. *Oh no – is he suddenly getting nervous?*

Jackson just made a mock-frightened face as he pointed at the sign for V-Gen Pharmaceuticals hanging on the wall opposite. 'Have you tricked me into being a test subject for some kind of funky experiment?'

'Of course not. Don't be silly!' Olivia pulled Jackson out of the elevator and towards the other side of the second-floor lobby, where the same mountainous security guard stood against the dark wall, guarding the entrance to ASHH. 'And, anyway, what would tests on you actually uncover? The secret to a million-dollar smile?'

Jackson laughed as they came to the centre of the lobby. *At least he's relaxed and prepared,* Olivia thought. When she'd undergone the Three Tests herself she hadn't known what she was in for. But this time she'd given Jackson as many hints as she dared.

She still shuddered when she remembered the Test of Darkness. She'd had to spend an entire night in a coffin! Then, in the Test of Faith, she'd been told by all the vamps that Ivy had abandoned her. It had been a horrible moment, but her faith in her sister had won her through. The Test of Blood had sounded the scariest to her at the time, but it had actually been the easiest. All she'd had to do was read the Blood Oath out loud, promising to keep the secret, and then have her fingertip pricked to sign in blood.

The security guard stepped aside to let them in, but his suspicious gaze followed Olivia through the door. She ignored him, focusing instead on how relaxed and calm Jackson was . . .

. . . until they stepped into the usual meeting room, and Jackson gasped.

Valencia Deborg sat at the long meeting table, facing them . . . and without her contacts her eyes glowed a fiery red.

Jackson didn't say a word. But as Olivia watched, his throat shifted in a convulsive swallow.

'So, Mr Caulfield.' Ms Deborg's face was as still as a statue. 'Are you ready?'

Jackson's fingers tightened around Olivia's, but he looked directly into the secretary's red eyes as he answered. 'Definitely.'

A wave of pride swept through Olivia as she looked at his easy grin. She knew her boyfriend was using all of his acting skill to hide his nerves . . . but no one else would ever have guessed from the way he looked now. *And he's doing all of this for me.* She gave him a warm smile, ignoring the secretary's glower.

'Hmm.' Ms Deborg tapped her long blood-red fingernails against the meeting table. The clicking noise echoed through the room. 'So, you've been told about the Tests, yes?'

'He has,' Charles said quietly. 'Jackson understands exactly what the consequences may be.'

'Excellent.' Ms Deborg gave a curt nod.

116

'Then – if he truly understands the danger – let the Tests begin.'

Wait! Suddenly, Olivia had to fight for breath.

She'd thought that she was prepared for this, but now she did not want to let go of her boyfriend's hand – as if by keeping hold of him, she could somehow keep him safe.

What if all those awful consequences actually *happened?* What if he didn't pass the Tests? He wouldn't just stop loving her – he'd start actively *disliking* her. How was she supposed to accept that?

'It's OK, Olivia,' Jackson whispered. He gently pulled his hand free of hers. 'I got this.'

Of course you do, Olivia thought. There was no way Jackson was going to fail, not after he had so brilliantly taken the Strange Truth in stride.

He's going to ace these Tests!

Jackson had told her he was more than ready for them – even the First Test, the one that Olivia had found the most frightening. He wasn't a bit worried about spending a night in a coffin. After all the time he'd spent in a water tank for the scuba-diving scenes in *The Groves*, a coffin was surely going to be a piece of cake. In fact he had such terrible jet-lag from all the time he'd spent flying between LA and Franklin Grove just lately that he was pretty sure he'd just go to sleep the minute that the lid shut and closed him in!

Olivia gave a real smile to Jackson. 'You're going to do great, I just know it.'

'I'm glad you both have so much faith,' Ms Deborg purred. 'But I must warn you that Jackson's Trials are to be *updated* versions of the ones that young Olivia undertook last year.'

What? Olivia's eyes flared wide open, all of her confidence draining away. She jerked around, but her father looked just as shocked as she felt . . .

'And so to the First Test,' said Ms Deborg. 'Olivia spent time in a simple coffin in an ordinary bedroom. But, using . . .' She cleared her throat, and looked straight at Olivia. '... *newly gathered* intelligence about Jackson's personal likes and dislikes, we've developed a new and improved version of the Test of Darkness. This time, it will take place in a mausoleum . . . and the entire place will be pitch black, all night.

Olivia saw Jackson's face turn pale underneath his California tan. *Wait,* she thought, *what does she mean by 'newly gathered intelligence'?*

Ms Deborg answered her question for her, looking straight at Jackson with unblinking red eyes. 'You *are* afraid of the dark, aren't you, Mr Caulfield? Well, think of this mausoleum as One Giant Coffin. Remember, facing your fears is one of the purest ways to prove your love.'

'How . . .' Jackson's voice cracked. He had to stop to clear his throat before he finished, his hands clenching and unclenching at his sides. 'How did you know I was afraid of the dark? I've never said that in any interviews.'

'We have ways of finding out secrets,' said Ms Deborg.

Jackson just stared at the secretary for a moment and Olivia's stomach dropped, as she waited for him to figure it out. His head whipped around. 'You *told* them?'

'I – I . . .' Olivia's hands went to her cheeks. She felt like such a fool. *That whole test Ms Deborg gave me was a trick!* I'm *the newly gathered intelligence!*

'I'm sorry, Jackson,' she said at last. 'I guess they tricked me.'

Ms Deborg looked straight at Jackson and her red eyes narrowed quizzically. 'How does this make you feel, Mr Caulfield? Do you feel as though you cannot trust your own girlfriend any more? Are you *quite* certain that you really want to be a part of our world, when we have the capability to find out anything we like about you?'

Jackson didn't answer for a long, tense moment. As Olivia watched the different emotions battle

120

across his face, her chest tightened. She could hardly breathe. *Has he lost his trust in me now?*

Finally, Jackson gave the secretary a firm nod. 'She was tricked. She didn't betray me. Let's do this.'

Ms Deborg just nodded and Olivia was finding it very annoying how hard it was to tell if she was pleased or angry. 'Very well,' said the secretary. 'Follow me.'

Standing up, she pressed her hand against the back wall of the meeting room and a hidden door swung open. Her jet-black high heels clacked against the floor as she disappeared through into the darkness.

'Here goes,' whispered Jackson and followed her through the door.

Olivia hurried after him, her father right behind. The narrow hallway was so dark she could barely keep from bumping into the walls, but her father steadied her every time, his vamp eyes handling the darkness just fine.

Finally, a red light glowed in the wall as an electric keypad lit up. By its faint glow Olivia could see that it was set into an imposing set of doors. Jackson stood just beside them, his shoulders squared.

Ms Deborg's fingernails flashed across the keypad and the doors slid open. 'The mausoleum,' she announced. Her red eyes glinted in the darkness. 'Why don't you make yourself comfortable, Jackson? Because you'll be in there for a very . . . long . . . time.'

Jackson ran a hand through his blond hair. It might have looked casual to someone who didn't know him, but Olivia knew very well that her boyfriend was starting to feel a little nervous. 'So, what's the deal?' he asked. 'I just sit in here?'

'That is correct,' said Ms Deborg. 'You must last the whole night, in the dark. There will be food and water inside, but you will have to feel your way to find it, obviously. And if you want to be let out at any time, you must call out a code word.'

'And what is the code word?' Olivia asked.

'Garlic bread.'

For a second Jackson just stared at Ms Deborg – then he burst out laughing, shaking his head. 'You vamps are funny.'

Then he turned back to Olivia, still laughing. He winked at her, before stepping through the open doors, into the utter blackness. Ms Deborg tapped the keypad once again.

The doors slid shut with a loud *boom* that seemed to shake the whole building. Olivia dreaded to think how loud it was inside the mausoleum.

Ms Deborg looked to Olivia and Charles. 'Perhaps don't make yourselves too comfortable . . .'

Olivia looked to her father, seeing him give her

a confident smile. She returned it, then aimed the smile at Ms Deborg.

'Jackson is going to be fine,' she said. 'Just you watch.'

Chapter Six

Ivy couldn't stop checking her phone the next morning as she sat with Brendan at the Meat and Greet. 'Ohh . . .' She tossed it down after her third check. *Still no texts!* 'I feel so bad I couldn't go with Olivia to the ASHH offices this morning! Stupid rules. I wanted to be there for her when Jackson gets out!'

Brendan made a face as he munched on his extra-salted fries. 'You think he'll make it through the whole night?'

'Of course! We would have heard by now if he'd failed, right?'

Brendan nodded his agreement. 'I can't believe

how much harder they've made those trials. Seriously. How do they expect any bunnies to ever pass?'

'Well . . .' Ivy began. But a whispered voice from across the diner caught her attention before she could finish.

'. . . that Ivy Vega girl *definitely* knew something!'

What? Ivy's head swivelled around. In the corner of her eye, she could see Brendan looking up, too, his own vamp hearing obviously catching the same set of whispers from the three girls who huddled across the room.

It's Fleur from Music Theory, Ivy realised. Fleur was with her friend Eva and another ninth-grade bunny, Mina, and her voice dropped even lower as she continued. 'So I checked into all those claims about Mr Hawkins being in a rock band, and guess what? There was nothing! Not a single rock band with a "Tommy Hawkins", *or* a Tom or a Thomas. I even looked to see if there were any "Tom-Toms"!

126

You know something, guys? I don't think he was a famous rock star.'

Mina gasped. 'Ooh, intriguing! But . . . did you think of looking for a "Tom Hawkins"?'

Fleur rolled her eyes. 'Didn't you just hear me say I didn't find that name?'

'No, no, no.' Mina shook her head. 'Not "Tom Hawkins", Fleur. "*Tom* Hawkins"!'

'Argh!' Fleur turned to look beseechingly at Eva. 'Are you hearing this?'

I wish I wasn't. Ivy stifled a groan. *Super-hearing is not always a gift!*

Across from her, Brendan's shoulders were shaking and he'd clapped one hand to his mouth to hold back his laughter. Ivy gave him a death-squint. *This isn't funny! We're probably losing IQ points with every second that we have to listen to this drivel!*

'But seriously,' Mina continued, '*did* you check for a *Tom* Hawkins?'

'Argh!' Fleur slammed one hand down on their

127

table. 'Are you concussed or something? How many times do I have to repeat myself?'

'I don't mean T-O-M,' Mina said. 'I mean, Thom with an "H". *Thom*. That's a name, too.'

'I have never, *ever* heard of that version.' Fleur groaned. 'Honestly. Thom with an "H"? That's almost as out-there as calling your child "Mina".'

'What?' Mina's gasp was so high-pitched, it hurt Ivy's ears. 'There's nothing wrong with my name. It's a classic!'

Fleur laughed. 'Maybe back in the Dark Ages.'

Mina laughed back and Ivy was a little relieved that this was just a couple of friends teasing each other, rather than typical mean girl-ness. But still . . . she did not want to have to listen to this. *If only there was a market where I could buy back moments of my life . . .*

Nope – here came Mina's voice again. 'What's the big deal about Mr Hawkins, anyway? Does it really matter whether or not he was really in a rock band?'

'Of course it matters!' Fleur said. 'Mr Hawkins used his so-called "rock experience" to get respect from the class for a *silent* music class, of all things. Have you seen the students coming out of his class lately? They're always talking about how great it is – whispering, of course, because they Respect the Silence.'

Ivy shared a look with Brendan, seeing in his eyes that he thought this was as weird as she did.

'In fact,' Fleur was saying now, 'I'm not sure I've seen him play an instrument. Do you think . . .? OK, this is going to sound crazy, but what if . . .? What if he lied on his job application? What if he's *not* a musician at all?'

Brendan leaned across the table, mumbling quietly. 'What do you think?'

Ivy shook her head. 'He wasn't lying when he talked about playing in concerts,' she told him. 'So he *can* play. But . . . I agree with Fleur, something's up.'

'And to think –' Fleur's voice cut into Ivy's ear like a blade – 'if it wasn't for Ivy Vega, we would never have had any idea!'

Brendan snickered softly and poked Ivy's arm. 'That's right,' he whispered. 'This whole conversation would never be happening without you.'

'Ugh. Don't remind me!' Ivy mumbled back.

'But how did she *know*?' Eva asked her friends. 'I mean, seriously. What was going on there?'

'She must have a real gift for reading people,' Fleur said.

'Ooh . . .' Mina drummed her fingers on the table, excited. 'Do you think she might be psychic?'

'Aaaand I'm done.' Ivy rolled her eyes at Brendan as she slid out of the booth. 'Time to nip this in the bud before it gets any worse.'

'Where are you going?'

Ivy drained her glass. 'Oh, look – I suddenly need a refill.'

'Hmm.' Brendan's eyebrows rose as he glanced

at the drinks machine. 'And . . . that just happens to be right next to the Gossip Gang. So what's your real plan?'

Ivy shrugged. 'I'll figure something out.'

'Got it.' Brendan winked. 'Don't worry. Just let them spend lots and lots of time with you. Then they'll *really* see you're nothing special.'

'Very funny.' Ivy gave him a playful kick under the table.

The sound of his laughter followed her as she walked across the room.

It was easy enough to refill her glass, but by the time she'd finished she still hadn't figured out *how* she was going to put a stop to the girls' gossip. As she glanced across the room and caught sight of Brendan grinning mischievously at her, her shoulders slumped.

Well, stake it! I'm going to have to follow his advice after all!

It was time to sit down, spend some time with

the gossiping trio, and show them all just how "normal" she really was . . . but she had a horrible feeling that Brendan was going to tease her about this for the next two months!

She could feel him watching her as she turned around and pretended to notice Fleur, Mina and Eva for the first time. 'Oh hi, guys!' She gave them a little wave as she walked over to their table. 'Do you mind if I join you? The thing is . . .' She bit back a mischievous grin of her own as she continued, knowing that every word was being carried back to Brendan's ears. 'My boyfriend is being *so boring* right now, you wouldn't believe it. He just keeps going on and on about his favourite TV show.' She rolled her eyes dramatically. 'Can you believe he actually watches *Shadowtown*?'

'No!' Eva giggled. 'Seriously?'

Mina made a face. 'Ewww!'

'Oh. My. Gosh.' Fleur shook her head in horror.

'You'd better sit down here and take a break. Boys can be so weird.'

'Oh yeah.' Ivy slid into the seat next to Mina and smiled with satisfaction . . . even as she heard Brendan's ultra-low whisper from across the room:

'You will *so* pay for that one, Vega!'

'Actually . . .' Fleur leaned across the booth table. 'I'm glad you're here. I've been wanting to tell you: you were right! Mr Hawkins was definitely not a rock star. He is *so* totally up to something with all those big stories about his past! But you're the only one who spotted him as a liar from the start.'

'Yeah, Ivy,' Mina leaned close to her, peering at her as if she were a strange specimen in a zoo. 'How did *you* see right through Mr Hawkins? That was amazing!'

'Oh, well . . .' Ivy shrugged uncomfortably, inching away as subtly as she could. Her brain was going at a hundred miles an hour now, which was exactly what she didn't want. *I came here to nip this in the bud,* she scolded herself, *not get intrigued all over again.* 'Lucky guess, really.'

'Hmph.' Fleur snorted, rattling her fingers against the table. 'It's all very mysterious, though, isn't it? How does a school like this end up hiring a possible fake? And why would anyone want to *pretend* to be a music teacher?'

Eva winced. 'Maybe he's upset that he never became a musician.'

He is *a musician,* Ivy thought. *He wasn't lying about that – but he has been lying about* something.

She shook her head, trying not to get sucked in. 'Don't over-think it, you guys,' she said. 'Remember, the fact that you haven't found any evidence that he was a rock star doesn't mean he wasn't one. What if he used a stage name?'

Mina's eyes widened, excited. 'Oooh, I hadn't thought of that.'

'Neither did I.' Fleur looked thoughtful.

Ivy bit her bottom lip. *I'm just making this worse – the girls are even more intrigued now . . . and so am I!*

'A lot of singers do that,' Eva said.

'Well, if she *is* right,' Fleur said, 'Mr Hawkins must have a *very interesting* reason to have changed his name.' She looked at Ivy so solemnly that Ivy almost laughed. 'Thank you. I appreciate you helping us with your . . . *skills.*'

Mina nodded gravely, while Eva bit her lip and watched Ivy with a worried expression.

Oh my darkness. That's not what I wanted! Ivy fought to keep a scowl off her own face. 'Look,' she began, 'I just –'

'I still sleep with a nightlight!' Eva blurted.

All three of the other girls swivelled around to stare at her. '*What?*' Ivy said.

Mina and Fleur exchanged wide-eyed looks.

Eva swallowed visibly. 'I just thought I'd better get it out there myself, before you do your mind-reading thing. Besides, I know Ivy saw through

135

my excuse the other day, about why I cancelled the sleepover.'

Fleur gasped like she'd been staked. 'You mean, your parents weren't fighting?'

Eva laughed. 'My parents *never* fight. It's actually ridiculous how pleasant they always are. I was just . . . a little embarrassed about the sleeping situation. But I'll tell you right now, that is *all* there is to find out about me!'

Bu-bu-bump! Bu-bu-bump! Ivy's truth-sense quivered as she sensed Eva's heart beating triple-time. The girl was *so* lying about how many embarrassing secrets she was keeping . . . but luckily, since Ivy couldn't read minds, she couldn't dig out any other ones even if she wanted to. She grimaced, scooting back in her chair. 'Seriously . . .'

'All right, all right,' Mina squeaked. 'I might as well confess – I have kind of a crush on Devon Drake!'

The other girls gasped. '*Devon?*' Eva demanded. 'Really?'

Fleur shook her head. 'You're kidding! The Dungeons & Dragons nerd?'

'Yeah, so?' Mina squared her shoulders, her cheeks bright pink. 'I'm just getting the truth out there for the same reason as Eva did. I don't want Ivy digging it out of my head!'

Ivy slapped one hand to her forehead in despair. 'Guys . . .'

But she was too late. Fleur yelped, 'I DON'T LIKE CHOCOLATE!'

'What?' Ivy slapped a hand to her forehead in disbelief. *This is not happening to me.*

'No!' Mina said. 'It isn't even *possible* not to like chocolate . . . is it?'

'But why would it be an embarrassing secret?' said Eva.

'Well, *I* don't know.' Fleur shrugged haughtily. '*I* think chocolate tastes disgusting. But apparently, everyone else in the world loves it, so it *has* to be weird for me not to like it. Right?'

'Oh, yes,' Mina said solemnly, her eyes wide. 'That is *so weird*, Fleur. And wow, just think: if it weren't for Ivy's special mindreading powers, Eva and I would never have known that truth about you!'

I can't believe this. Ivy let her head *thunk* down on the table. Brendan's muffled laughter rang in her ears, but she couldn't even summon up a snarl for him. *Mission: ... what's the opposite of 'accomplished'? Not only did I not distract the girls from my 'psychicness', but I'm now the Queen of Gossip. This could not have gone worse. My new ninth sense bites!*

I'm actually a little bored, Olivia thought, as she sat in the corridor outside the mausoleum that morning. She was surprised to find that she thought boredom was a good thing – it meant that she definitely, definitely wasn't worried about Jackson's chances of passing the First Test.

The lights in the corridor had been turned

on this time, lighting the narrow passageway with a dim glow. She was sitting with her bio-dad and step-mom on spindly chairs, while Ms Deborg stood across from them in her elegant black and red kimono. Her hands were clasped in front of her, totally calm, and she was as still as a statue, again.

At this time on a Saturday morning the whole second floor was deserted. Their small group was the only one in the building and every tiny creaking sound seemed so loud Olivia almost felt like she had vampire hearing.

'How much longer, do you think?' she whispered to her bio-dad.

'It can't be too much longer,' Charles told her. He looked at his elegant gold watch and frowned. 'By my reckoning . . . Jackson has spent more than sixteen hours in ASHH's mausoleum-set.'

'Wow,' said Olivia, impressed that her boyfriend had not shouted out the ridiculous safe word –

especially when he had such a powerful fear of the dark . . .

A high-pitched beep suddenly sounded from the keypad on the wall nearby, and the big metal doors slid open.

'Jackson!' Olivia leaped to her feet and started towards the mausoleum, but then skidded to a stop.

He was bleary-eyed and wild-haired as he came stumbling out of the darkness, grimacing as he held his hand up to shield his face from the dim light outside.

'Olivia?' he croaked. 'Is that you?'

Olivia threw her arms around her boyfriend. 'Are you OK?' she asked.

'Oh yeah, totally,' he said, through a scrunched-up face. 'I'm all good.'

'Are you sure?'

He pressed his cheek against her hair. 'Yes,' he said. 'Don't worry.' But his voice kind of shook and Olivia looked back to her bio-dad. Charles didn't

140

seem all that concerned, so Olivia told herself to calm down.

It's not like anybody *would actually* enjoy *what Jackson has just been through.*

She turned back to Jackson. 'Let's go home,' she said. 'I'll get you some breakfast, and you can shower, and then –'

'Ahem.' Ms Deborg cleared her throat. 'That was just the First Test,' she said drily. 'Now begins the Second.'

'What?' Jackson finally opened his eyes properly, staring at the secretary. 'Don't I even get a rest period?'

'You didn't take the opportunity to sleep?' Ms Deborg asked. 'You had all night.'

Jackson laughed, but Olivia thought she detected a note of nervousness underneath it. 'Man, you vamps really make us earn it, huh? It's not enough to make me sit in the dark and listen to sounds of creepy-crawlies scuttling everywhere. Oh, and – by

141

the way – those sound effects were *killer.*'

Olivia felt her jaw clench – Jackson was kind of rambling. The First Test had bothered him more than he was going to admit.

But Ms Deborg's face showed no emotion. It was as if Jackson was talking to a robot. 'Now comes the Test of Faith.'

Olivia remembered her own Test of Faith, when she'd refused to believe that Ivy would abandon her.

How had the Vampire Round Table made *this* Test harder?

Half an hour later Olivia was sitting next to Jackson in the back of a moving hearse, with her bio-dad and stepmom sitting across from them. The windows were tinted too dark for any of them to see the landscape moving past. Jackson was looking a little better than he had when he came out of the mausoleum, but not much.

Olivia tucked her arm through his. 'Hey,' she whispered, sliding closer to him on the black cushioned seat. 'Are you OK?'

'Oh yeah,' Jackson gave her a thumbs up. Then he sighed. 'Actually, between you and me, last night was super scary. I haven't eaten or slept, and I'm in the back of a hearse surrounded by vampires. I kind of should be curled up in a ball, crying for my mom right now! But I'm made of stern stuff. I just . . . wonder what they've got planned for me next.'

Olivia looked across at her parents. 'Do you guys know where Ms Deborg is sending us?'

Lillian shook her head. So did Charles, his voice heavy. 'It's better that you two don't know ahead of time. You'd only worry more if you knew.'

The hearse finally slowed to a stop about twenty minutes later. When Charles opened the door the bright autumn sunlight felt almost blinding. Olivia blinked and blinked again as she stepped out of the hearse into . . .

'A cornfield?' she said blankly.

The first snow had melted a few days ago and a bright November sun shone down, but most of the tall pale stalks that still covered the giant field looked like bleak survivors in a desolate landscape. In the centre of the field, though, a massive square of bushy, ripe-looking stalks rose close together, higher than Olivia's head and extending for what looked like a quarter-mile in each direction.

That really doesn't look natural for November, Olivia thought uneasily. *I wonder if V-Gen's gotten involved with this Test?*

'The Second Test,' Ms Deborg drawled, appearing from the rustling mass of corn. In her brightly coloured kimono, she looked as out of place against the bleak farmland.

Just how old is she, anyway? Olivia wondered. Obviously, no matter when the vamp secretary had been born, she had found a fashion that worked for her and stuck with it.

'The *new* Test of Faith,' Ms Deborg continued, 'requires Jackson to make it from one side of this cornfield to another. Through this maze . . . of maize!'

She gave a soft chuckle, and Olivia fought the urge to roll her eyes. This was pretty much the first show of emotion from Ms Deborg since she'd come back into their lives, and it was at her own – terrible – joke!

Jackson looked at Olivia, his nose wrinkling. He always made that face when he was confused. *I wish the VRT had asked me about his facial expressions. I know all of them.*

'How is that a test of "faith"?' Jackson asked Ms Deborg.

'Because,' said the secretary, 'you won't only have to worry about finding your way through the maze. At numerous points in your journey you will also discover some . . . *special* challenges. These have been designed especially for you, Jackson . . .'

She looked right at Olivia. 'We had to do some special research to make sure we tailored this maze to you.'

Oh no! Olivia sensed Jackson swinging round to look sharply at her. But she was too busy to apologise again, as she aimed a death-squint worthy of Ivy at her grouchiest straight at Ms Deborg's smug face. 'This isn't fair,' she said. 'You've made these Tests harder just because I passed them last year. Haven't you? But bunnies have to win sometimes, you know!'

'I'm glad you think that,' said Ms Deborg. 'Because, for this Test, you'll be right alongside Jackson, trying to help him "win".'

Wait a minute. Olivia traded a confused look with Jackson. *The VRT wouldn't want us to help each other. What's really going on?*

'Ohhh.' Olivia swallowed hard. *Now I get it.* 'So that's why it's a Test of *Faith*. You want to see if the two of us will really stick together when things get bad.'

Normally she would have said, *Of course we can!*

But with the way that the VRT were making these Tests harder, she wasn't *as* confident as she would normally be.

Olivia looked up at Jackson. 'Ready?' she asked.

Jackson flashed his famous smile. It had been discounted down from a million dollars, but was still pretty expensive. 'Ready.'

'The maze begins *there,*' Ms Deborg said, pointing to the bushy square of tall cornstalks that she'd stepped out of, 'and it ends at the far end of the square.'

Olivia had to almost jog to keep with Jackson as he marched towards the six-foot-high Maze of Maize.

Together they stepped into a narrow path that had been cut through the rustling cornstalks, leading them one way and then another, until Olivia had nearly lost all memory of which way they had come from in the first place. At every turning there were new paths they could take. As they reached another one, they hesitated for a moment, both trying to decide which way to go. Olivia tensed with frustration. She couldn't even listen out for clues that might direct them, because the only sound was the wind rustling through the high cornstalks . . .

. . . until a high-pitched squeaking sound broke out just behind them.

A river of mice flooded down the aisle, moving so quickly Olivia didn't even have time to jump aside before they began scuttling in a rippling mass over the toes of her pink boots.

'Come on!' Jackson yanked her away, leaping over the river of mice and pulling her down the next turning, away from the scuttling rodents.

'Is this the way out?' Olivia asked breathlessly, as she ran with him.

148

'Who cares?' As he finally slowed to a walk, with one final nervous glance back at the path behind them, her boyfriend's face looked paler than ever. 'As long as there aren't any mice in this direction . . .'

Of course. He's terrified of them . . . and the VRT know it. Olivia winced. She wanted to put her arm around him in a hug, but from the tense way he was holding himself she wasn't sure her gesture would be welcome.

Because of me, Jackson just had to outrun a river of mice, she thought glumly. *What could be worse?*

CRASH!

Olivia spun around, following the noise . . . and gulped. *Uh-oh.*

Three tall figures had just lurched out of the living walls of the maze, into the path behind them . . . and all three of them wore big white grinning clown masks.

'*Hahahahaha!*' they all cackled in unison.

149

Jackson went into full-on Bug-Out Mode, bolting forwards almost vampirically fast, dragging Olivia with him and forcing her to sprint to keep up.

'Oof!' She stumbled and nearly fell, but managed to catch her balance just in time.

Jackson took one turning after another without a moment's hesitation, not paying attention to where they were going – he just seemed intent on getting away from the clowns who were still chasing after them, their eerie laughter echoing through the maze.

Finally the haunting sound faded into the distance. 'Whew.' Olivia pulled Jackson to a halt, laughing with all the scant breath she had left. 'I . . . can't believe . . . we just ran like that . . . from clowns!' She shook her head, grinning, as she bent over to grab her knees, panting. 'Seriously, Jackson. I know you're afraid of them . . . but you know they weren't *actually* going to hurt us, right?'

'*What?*' Jackson rounded on her, scowling. 'Are you actually making fun of me? *Now?*'

'No!' Blinking, Olivia straightened. 'Jackson, I just thought it was funny how –'

'Funny?' Jackson demanded. 'This isn't *funny* . . .' He fell quiet, staring at her for a long moment.

'What?' Olivia asked.

'Is that why you told the vampires about all of my worst fears?' he asked. 'Because you thought it would be funny to watch me freaking out like this?'

'No!' Olivia gasped. 'How could you ask me that? Do you think I would ever do that to you?'

Jackson just stared at the ground, shaking his head. 'Well, you told them how I didn't do well in the dark . . .'

Olivia's mouth dropped open, but no words would come. She didn't know what to say to that. Instead, she turned around and stomped off down the path ahead of them, her pink boots crunching hard against the dirt. She was so mad at him right now – how could he think that she would help the VRT make fun of him? Did he not know her at all?

A moment later Jackson fell into step beside her. But he didn't make any move to take her hand and Olivia didn't offer it.

They might as well have been a million miles away from each other for all the closeness that she felt. *So much for the Test of Faith.*

Olivia sighed as they came up to the next turning. She snuck a glance at Jackson. He looked as miserable as she felt.

He's not the only one who said something mean just now, she thought unhappily.

And from the look on his face, she wasn't the only one feeling bad about their argument either.

Her steps slowed as they neared the turning. 'Jackson . . .' she began.

'Olivia.' He turned towards her, reaching out as if to take her hand. 'Look, I wanted to say –'

'*Raaaaaaaow!*' A giant orange . . . *creature* leaped

around the corner, baring massive white teeth and claws and lashing a furry tail.

'Ahhhhh!' Olivia couldn't help it. Even as she heard Jackson's own shout of surprise, she was already recoiling – and when she saw the creature readying itself to pounce, she turned and fled. *Those teeth . . . those claws!* Panic boiled through her as she fled, fighting her way through thick walls of corn and losing all track of paths and direction. *Ohmygosh, ohmygosh, ohmygoshohmygosh – terrifying cat monster. Terrifying CAT MONSTER!*

It took several moments after the creature's yowls had faded into the distance before she finally managed to force herself to stop running.

Wait, cat monster?! What am I even talking about?

Franklin Grove was home to some pretty weird creatures, but cat monsters were definitely not among them . . . which meant that had to have been just a vampire in a suit. If she'd only taken the time to look more closely, she probably would have seen that it wasn't even a convincing costume.

'Whew.' Half-laughing, she leaned against the closest prickly wall of corn and closed her eyes. 'I ... guess that was kind of ridiculous, wasn't it?' she mumbled.

'Oh well.' She shook her head, aiming her rueful words at Jackson. 'I guess at least we're even now, right? Because that one definitely scared us both.'

Jackson didn't answer. All she heard was the rustling corn.

Uh-oh. Olivia opened her eyes. 'Jackson? Where'd you go?'

She stood alone in a narrow aisle of the maze. Her boyfriend was nowhere to be seen.

Olivia sucked in a breath. 'Jackson!' Her legs burned from all the running that she had done already, but she ignored the pain as she tore up and down the empty paths. 'Jackson!' she yelled. '*Jackson!*'

It was no use.

Ten minutes later she finally sank to the ground, groaning and tipping her head into her hands.

Why did I ever let go of his hand?

I guess the Test of Faith is over. Tears burned at her eyes, but she refused to give in to them. There would be time enough to cry later on . . . when all her boyfriend's sweet memories of her had been turned sour.

Blinking hard, she gazed around her at the tall, rustling walls of corn . . . then sighed and pulled out her phone from the pocket of her coat. *I bet the VRT probably have rules against me calling him, but so what? This is the modern world, after all!*

She turned the phone on.

'Oh *no!*' She groaned again, even more deeply, as she looked at the blinking icon at the top. *No signal!*

Her chest tightened at the thought. It was bad enough for her to be trapped here, but at least this maze wasn't filled with her worst fears.

What must Jackson be feeling right now?

And shouldn't she have heard him by now, no matter how far they'd run from each other?

What if his fear had taken over? For all she knew he could be curled up in a ball somewhere in the maze right now, completely paralysed by panic.

I can't leave him here alone, no matter what. Slipping the phone back into her coat pocket, Olivia pushed herself up. This time she didn't run up and down the rustling aisles of the maze. She walked slowly and carefully, doing her best to listen . . . but it was no good. *If only I had Ivy's vamp-hearing! Or her sense of smell . . .*

Ten minutes later, she was trudging down another path. Mice ran over her feet, but she barely noticed. A clown leaped out in front of her and she simply lowered her head and hurried past. She was running again by the time she reached the next turn. She whirled around it and –

BUMP! She ran straight into a moving figure.

'Aah!' She leaped back, screaming.

Warm hands closed around her upper arms, stopping her before she could flee. 'Olivia!' Jackson gave her a long desperate look, then threw his arms around her and squeezed her tight. 'I'm so glad you're OK!'

Olivia hugged him back. 'I've been looking *everywhere* for you.'

'I was worried you might be lost in here, not able to get out . . .' His voice broke off as he shook his head, ruffling her hair with his chin.

'I'm fine,' she said, 'just a bit disorientated.'

'That's OK,' he told her. 'I found the way out.'

Olivia let her head fall back in relief. 'Thank goodness! You can show me the way while we – Jackson?' She blinked as he tightened his grip on her. 'Are you OK?'

'No,' he said quietly. 'I'm not. Olivia, I am so sorry about what I said earlier. I know you would never have told the vamps about my fears on purpose.'

'Jackson . . .'

'I was just – I was trying to deflect from how scared I was,' he finished in a rush. 'But I know it wasn't cool for me to act like that. I'm sorry.'

'That's OK.' Olivia reached out to cup his face in her hands. 'I understand,' she said softly. 'And I'm sorry, too. I should never have made fun of your fears.'

'Thank you.' He hugged her tightly, then finally let her go with a sigh. 'Let's get out of here!'

With Jackson leading the way, it was only five more minutes before they emerged through the door-shaped arch that had been cut into the far end of the maze wall. As they walked, Olivia wondered if their almost-argument would count as failing the Test.

'Thank darkness!' Lillian hurried forwards to hug them both, followed by a relieved-looking Charles.

'Well done, you two,' he said. Standing beyond

158

Olivia's parents, Ms Deborg gave a condescending nod and smile. 'Young Jackson has completed *both* parts of the Test.'

'*Both* parts?' Jackson frowned as Lillian stepped back. 'What was the second part?'

Charles's voice was quiet but intense. 'By braving your own deepest fears to go back and find Olivia, even when you had the opportunity to escape yourself, you proved that you are someone in whom my daughter – and by extension, our whole community – can place faith.'

Of course they can! Olivia reached out and took Jackson's hand. He squeezed it back, and they smiled at each other.

'Just one more Test to go,' she whispered. 'You've got this!'

Chapter Seven

As Ivy walked towards the school cafeteria for lunch on Monday, she could see Sophia talking beside her, mouth moving and hands gesturing enthusiastically. But Ivy couldn't hear a single word that her best friend was saying through the thick wad of cotton wool that she'd stuffed into her ears five minutes earlier. She had to protect herself from the truth somehow!

Why is this whole school so full of liars?

The cotton-wool defence had been her final hope ... but when Sophia stepped directly in front of her, pulling a face and mouthing: '*Earth to Ivy? Seriously, I'm pouring my heart out here and you look like someone just cancelled* Shadowtown!' she had to give it up.

Ivy took the cotton wool out of her ears.

'Whoa.' Sophia started laughing as she stared at the white wads in Ivy's hands. 'Has it really gotten that bad?'

Ivy sighed. 'Just watch this,' she said glumly, and stepped through the door of the noisy, crowded cafeteria.

The moment that she entered, silence fell. All across the cafeteria heads swivelled as students turned to stare at her in worried fascination.

'Ivy!' Fleur jumped up from the nearby table that she shared with Mina and Eva, and beckoned urgently. 'Have you had any more insights into Mr Hawkins?'

Ivy rolled her eyes. 'No, I haven't. And honestly, what's the big deal?'

Fleur looked outraged. 'It is a big deal if a teacher is being dishonest.'

161

'Right,' Eva agreed, beside her. 'But more importantly . . . what else have you found out? You know, about other people? Anything good?'

'Huh?' Ivy stepped back.

But now Mina was staring at her hopefully, too. 'You must have found out some really interesting secrets, mustn't you? With your special powers?'

'I don't have powers,' said Ivy, looking for an escape route. 'Except the power of hunger. I'm really hungry, you guys. So if you don't mind, I'm going to get some lunch now.'

She turned on her heel and marched to the end of the lunch line, with Sophia snickering behind her.

'Admit it,' Sophia said as they joined the line. 'That wasn't *so* bad. You have been popular before, remember?'

'Yeah, but back when I was the Popular Goth of Ninth Grade, at least that was because people thought I was cool. This time . . .' Ivy scowled, 'they just like me for the gossip. And those that don't want gossip from me are just scared of me.'

'I doubt that,' Sophia protested.

'Oh really? Watch this.' Ivy stepped forwards, tapping the shoulder of the ninth-grade jock who stood ahead of her in line, still wearing running shorts despite the November weather. 'Hey Sal.'

Sal turned around, his eyes bugging out when he saw her. 'Ivy!'

'How's it going?' she asked cheerfully.

Sal's eyes got even wider with panic. 'Uhhh . . .'

She gave him a happy smile. 'So, how much did last week's English homework bite?'

'Uhhh . . . I have no opinions on the English homework. None whatsoever.' As the line moved forwards, Sal nearly leaped the extra six inches away from her, eyeing her like she was a dangerous animal.

Ivy turned back to Sophia and dropped her voice back to a whisper. 'You see? Either people want to use me as their personal psychic . . . or else they're scared to say a word to me in case I catch them in a lie and tell everyone else about it! The only ones who don't fit either of those categories are the guitar fanatics who idolise Mr Hawkins so much. And they hate me for "denying the truth about him".' She rolled her eyes.

'Poor Ivy.' Smiling, Sophia shook her head. 'At least you don't have to worry about anyone intentionally lying to you for a while, though . . .'

As they crossed the crowded cafeteria a moment later, conversations went silent all around them, groups of students turning one by one to cast nervous looks at Ivy as she walked past. Ivy's shoulders were tense with irritation by the time they reached their usual table and she was grinding her teeth. *I'd love to show them some real special powers . . .*

Thank darkness her real friends hadn't changed. Skateboard-king Finn just gave her an easy smile as he continued his lecture to Brendan about the fine details of exactly how he'd designed his latest skate routine ... and Ivy didn't need to be a walking lie-detector to see that her boyfriend was about to fall asleep if the conversation didn't change soon.

She slid into her chair, suddenly missing her twin. If Olivia were here, she knew she'd have an easier time relaxing ... but Olivia was holed up in the library, getting all of her homework done during lunch so that she'd be able to spend all her time with Jackson after school.

Still, that didn't mean Ivy had to just sit around feeling annoyed, did it? She turned to her best friend. 'Do you want to hang out after school?' she asked. 'I'm pretty sure Lillian got the latest issue of *VAMP* magazine this morning and she'd probably let you borrow it.'

That offer would usually have made Sophia leap to attention. Right now, though, Sophia's narrow eyebrows were drawn together as she frowned at the nearest window.

Ivy followed her best friend's gaze and sighed.

Mr Hawkins was walking just outside with two seniors who were gazing at him like he was sharing all the secrets of life . . . and just behind them was AJ, Sophia's crush.

Oh my darkness. Ivy rolled her eyes as she saw the music teacher mime playing air guitar. Now she knew how he was keeping all three seniors so enthralled: he was telling them stories about his 'rock star' past! Everyone was falling for it, even though the air guitar was the only instrument . . .

Ivy's eyes narrowed. *It's the only instrument any of us have seen him play. If he wants to talk big about his past exploits, why not show off in class – where there are actual* instruments, *that make actual* music?

She'd been telling the truth to Fleur earlier: she did not care what Mr Hawkins had done with his life before he came here. But the more she thought about it, the less she could deny that he was hiding *something.*

Hate to admit it, but maybe Fleur's on to something after all.

It was a skill to be able to tell when someone was lying, but what good was that skill if you didn't know what they were lying about . . . or why they were lying in the first place?

It was time for Ivy Vega, investigative-journalist-in-training, to get to the bottom of this musical mystery.

Chapter Eight

'I just don't get it!' Jackson paced up and down the Abbotts' cosy living room that afternoon after school. 'Why haven't the VRT given me the Third Test yet? What are they up to? Are they just trying to make me even *more* nervous, or what?'

'I don't know.' Olivia shook her head unhappily as she curled up in one corner of the big plush blue sofa, wrapped up in a fluffy pink lap blanket that her adoptive mom had knitted. 'I thought it would be done by now, too.'

'Do you have any idea what they'll do to ramp up the Third Test?' Jackson asked.

'I have no idea,' Olivia admitted, nibbling on her

lower lip. The Third Test was the Test of Blood, and for her it had been just a prick of her finger, a signature in blood. Nowhere near as gruesome as it sounded.

She had a feeling that would not be the case today. Who knew what the VRT's new updated version would be? Judging by how drastically they'd expanded the first two Tests, she wouldn't be surprised if Jackson ended up having to peer at different blood samples and try to tell AB from O-negative.

Ewww! Just the idea of that was enough to make Olivia feel ill.

'What is it?' Jackson demanded. 'What are you trying not to tell me?' His face paled. 'Oh man, you think it's gonna be super gross, don't you?'

'No!' Olivia jumped up from the couch and put her hands on his shoulders to get him to stop pacing. 'Mine wasn't a gross one. And there's no reason yours will be, either. It's just –'

She broke off as the door to the living room opened and Mrs Abbott ducked in, carrying a huge box and looking nervously back over her shoulder. 'Olivia!' she whispered. 'Can I hide this box in your bedroom closet? It's your father's anniversary gift. I don't want him finding it before this weekend! He's going to flip out when he sees this yin-yang lava lamp!'

Aha! Olivia thought. So *that* was the plan her mom had been covering up last week when she'd set off Ivy's truth-sense alarm about Mr Abbott's catalogue!

'Of course you can, Mom.' She forced a smile. 'There's plenty of space.'

'Thanks, sweetie. I'll just ... Actually, hold on a minute.' Mrs Abbott paused in the middle of the doorway and looked from Olivia to Jackson, frowning. 'Is everything OK, you two? Because there seems to be a bit of an *atmosphere* in here right now.'

Oops. Olivia put on her sweetest smile. 'We were just running lines for *Eternal Sunset*,' she said. 'It's a really heavy scene, so . . .' She shrugged, pulling a rueful face.

'Gotcha.' Mrs Abbott rolled her eyes as she backed out, wrestling the big box through the doorway. 'I have to say, I will be glad when you two finally finish filming this movie. It feels like you've been shooting it for years!'

As the door fell closed behind her, Olivia gave a sigh of relief. She turned around and found Jackson frowning at her. 'What's wrong?'

'I . . .' He paused, looking undecided. 'Forget it.'

'Jackson?' Now Olivia was frowning, too. She stepped closer to him. 'What is it?'

He looked to the floor, sticking his hands in his jeans pockets and shifting backwards. 'It's just . . . you lied to your mom so easily.' He gave an unhappy shrug. 'And I guess I never realised before just how good you really are at concealing the truth.'

Ouch. Olivia wanted to protest ... but it was true. She *had* gotten really good at lying to the people she loved, ever since she'd found out the vampire secret.

'I have to do it,' she said quietly. 'And so will you, if you pass the Third Test. Lie by omission, at least. But it's for their own protection. Otherwise, they'd have to pass the Three Tests, too. Would you want to put your own parents through that?'

Jackson looked horrified. 'No way!'

'Exactly.' Olivia sank back down on to the sofa. 'And the vampires *need* to have their secret protected. If all the bunnies in the world found out the truth, there would be panic. Outrage. Scary stuff happening to innocent vamps.' She winced. 'We can't let that happen.'

'No, I get that. But still . . .' Jackson sat down at the other end of the sofa, frowning. 'You have to keep so much from them. Isn't it exhausting?'

Olivia leaped off the sofa with a gymnastic

twirl. 'Do I look exhausted?' she demanded. She summoned up her best cheerleading smile. 'Now, come on! Why don't we turn my lie into a truth? We might as well distract ourselves by running lines for the movie after all, don't you think?'

'Might as well.' Jackson gave a wry smile. 'If I'd known I'd be dealing with actual real-life vamps, I'd have asked for help with *Eternal Sunset* months ago!'

Olivia rolled her eyes. 'That wouldn't have done you any good,' she told him. 'This film is far too unrealistic for any of the Franklin Grove vamps to be any help. And my Transylvanian family . . .'

He stared at her, his mouth falling open. 'Are you serious? You have Transylvanian family? Do you, like . . . know Dracula?'

'I'll explain everything,' Olivia promised. 'After you've passed. But for now, let's distract ourselves.'

They threw themselves into the final scene of the movie with gusto – Irina, one of the two vampire twins Olivia played, was drawing her final breaths, after thousands of years of life. Olivia staggered up and down the room as Irina argued with Wesley, the reincarnated human twin she loved.

'Just take it!' Jackson demanded, chasing after her. 'Take my blood. It will save you!'

'I would . . . rather . . . die,' Olivia gasped.

'But you know it's the only way!'

Olivia spun around and grasped Jackson's shirt with both hands. '*All* I know,' she said, her voice throbbing with pain, 'is that I could never, ever cause you any harm. I've spent hundreds of years resisting the urge to bite every version of you that I've met, in every era of history. Do you really think I'd start now? Do you really think my own life means that much more to me than *yours*?'

Pulling free of her grip, Jackson dropped to his knees in front of her and yanked up his shirtsleeve to reveal one bare wrist. 'I'm begging you,' he said, his face set in anguish. 'Do this for me, not just for you. I don't care what it takes. I don't care about the pain. I just can't bear to watch you die! And even if I die, I know that I will live again. How can I live again if you're not there for me to find?'

Olivia swayed on her feet as Irina fought her final fall. 'My darling Wesley,' she whispered. 'I would do anything for you ... except hurt you. If I must die to protect you, then I ... will ... ahhh!'

Closing her eyes, she fell backwards in a swoon.

Olivia didn't even try to break her fall, knowing from earlier practice sessions that Jackson always, always caught her.

Thunk! Her head knocked against the carpeted floor as she fell flat on the ground.

'Ow!' Her eyes flew open. 'Jackson! What happened?'

'I'm so sorry!' Still crouched on his knees,

Jackson stared down at her, looking stunned. 'I got distracted.'

'Obviously.' Olivia grimaced as she rubbed her aching head. 'By what?'

'By you,' he said simply. 'Olivia, you weren't just acting in that scene, were you?'

Olivia's eyes widened as she stared back at him. 'What do you mean?'

'You were finding the truth in that moment,' Jackson said. 'I could tell. When Irina was swearing not to hurt Wesley . . . you really meant that, didn't you? For yourself . . . and for me, too.'

'Ohh,' Olivia breathed. She held his gaze as she sat up. 'I think you're right.' She shrugged. 'I might not have been doing it consciously, but . . . I know I've never *felt* that dialogue so strongly before.' She smiled weakly. 'I guess . . . it really felt like that scene had a lot of resonance for us right now, didn't it?'

'Because you're worried about hurting me?'

Jackson shook his head, taking her hand in his. 'Olivia, I know I said it was a shock to see how well you could lie when you need to . . . but there's one thing about you that I know for certain. You would never, *ever* hurt me! How could you even worry about that?'

Tears sparked behind Olivia's eyes as she looked into his beautiful blue gaze. 'Jackson, all those dreadful Tests . . . I'm the reason you're having to go through them.'

'And if you didn't believe, in your heart, that I could pass them, you would never have entered me into them,' he said firmly. 'I really understood that just now, when you were speaking as Irina. And for the very first time . . .' A dazzling grin broke across his face – the million-dollar smile was no longer on a discount. 'I have *no* doubts about that last Test any more. I know for a fact that I am going to pass it!'

Olivia wanted to be drawn into his enthusiasm,

but ... 'You know you can't be sure,' she told him miserably. 'After the way the first two Tests went, the third one is bound to be the toughest so far. And –'

'Shh.' Jackson stood up and pulled her to her feet. 'Olivia,' he said, as he wrapped her in a warm hug, 'I don't care how tough it is. It's just like Wesley said to Irina ... I'll do anything for you, no matter what it takes. The only thing I couldn't stand would be to lose you.' He squeeze her hand tight. 'So we're not going to let that happen.'

Chapter Nine

Ivy rolled her eyes as she saw the line of excited boys and girls in rock T-shirts all streaming towards the music wing after school. 'Seriously? They've *all* gotten sucked in by Mr Hawkins's stories?'

'It's his new after-school music club,' Sophia told her. '"Learn from an expert how to be a real rock star!"' She made finger quotes around the words, grimacing. 'Didn't you see the signs posted around the school?'

'I didn't,' Ivy said grimly, 'but I'm watching this now . . . and I think it needs some real investigation. Come on.'

'Really?' Sophia groaned. 'I'm not sure I can take a silent music club . . .'

But when they walked into the classroom a few minutes later, they found it full of noise, with guitars being strapped on in all directions and discordant power chords raging through the air.

Ouch! Ivy's sensitive vamp hearing was enough to stagger her to a stop in the doorway for a moment, as she fought to adjust to all the clashing sounds that battered at her ears. *This is vamp torture!*

Mr Hawkins, though, looked as if he was having the time of his life. He stood in the middle of the classroom, surrounded by three girls and three boys with guitars, listening patiently to all their different attempts and coaching them through their fingerings by showing them on his own guitar.

'Well, there goes the theory that he can't play an instrument,' Sophia murmured. Her gaze shifted to rest on AJ, who was holding a guitar and standing near Mr Hawkins.

'Apparently.' Ivy frowned as she picked out the sound of Mr Hawkins's mellow chords, as he showed the students what to do. 'He really is good at the guitar, isn't he?' Shaking her head, she forced herself into the noisy room. 'But it's worth being sure. My truth sense goes haywire whenever he mentions his rock past. Come on. You create a diversion while I sneak into his office!'

'Oh, trust me. I'll create a diversion!' Sophia strode across the room, flinging her long dark hair back from her face. Ivy hovered halfway across the room, watching her friend approach their teacher.

Would Sophia start asking him questions about rock fashion? Or . . .

Without even breaking her stride, Sophia reached out and yanked a spare electric guitar off a nearby chair. 'Can I join in?' she asked Mr Hawkins.

'Of course!' Mr Hawkins smiled as he waved an arm to point her towards a nearby amp and watched her plug in her guitar. 'Have you ever played before?'

'Oh . . .' Sophia grinned fiercely. 'Just a little.' She swept one hand down and the whole room fell silent as a wildly spectacular riff swept through the air.

'Wow!' AJ stared at her, mouth hanging open, as the final echoes of Sophia's playing faded.

'Well.' Mr Hawkins shook his head, a delighted grin breaking over his face. '*Well!* Let's see what we can do with that kind of talent!'

As he and all the other students converged in a circle around Sophia and her guitar, Ivy hurried through the open door into Mr Hawkins's office.

The tiny room was stuffed so full of sheet music and instruments, it was hard to even find a pathway through them. Still, she didn't let the sight intimidate her. *There's got to be something in here that will reveal the truth! If he really was in a famous band, he'd have some mementos with him. Musicians are often sentimental, aren't they?*

Keeping her vampire hearing attuned to the sound of his voice in the next room as he coached Sophia through more and more technically demanding riffs, she bent over his desk and started flipping through sheet music and student papers. Nothing suspicious.

She stepped back, her eyes trailing over the clutter on the teacher's desk. Maybe there wasn't going to be anything to find. Maybe, just this once, someone would reveal themselves to *not* be a lying liar.

That would be nice!!

Ivy leaned over and looked in the desk drawers – which she figured it was OK to do, because they were already open. She wasn't invading Mr Hawkins's privacy.

She rifled through the magazines and guitar picks inside. She forced herself to ignore the tug of guilt she felt. *This isn't just nosiness,* she told herself firmly. *Fleur has a point: if Mr Hawkins has been lying*

183

about being a rock star, he could be lying about his teaching qualifications, too!

So she wasn't just hunting to satisfy her curiosity, now . . . she might even be saving her school!

Aha. As she riffled through the final drawer, she felt something hard underneath the pile of music magazines. *What's this?*

Carefully, she pulled out a framed magazine cover . . . with Mr Hawkins in the centre of the photo.

Whoa! Ivy's eyebrows arched high as she took in the sight of her music teacher in luminous pink and yellow clothing, wearing a fuzzy orange wig and holding a broom in his arms as if it were a guitar. Around him, four other guys in eye-wateringly bright colours held everything from toasters to kettles as if they were different kinds of instruments. Bright pink letters at the top of the cover read: **Check out** Champions of Chores**, the latest album from our favourite children's**

novelty band: The Zig-Zaggers!

Ivy gasped. *So that's it!* Now she knew why her truth-sense had gone off.

Mr Hawkins had been in a professional band, all right . . . but it hadn't been a rock band!

'What do you think you doing?' Mr Hawkins snapped, from the doorway.

Argh – busted! Ivy nearly dropped the frame as she stumbled back. She'd been so intent on her search, she'd forgotten to keep an ear out. *I guess he really* does *know the meaning of silence . . .*

Her music teacher was red-faced with fury. 'What is the meaning of this *trespassing*?' he sputtered.

'I – um . . .' Ivy began.

But before she could even come up with an excuse, Mr Hawkins crossed the tiny room in two quick, gliding steps.

I should have known, Ivy realised, as he yanked the framed cover from her hands. From the very

185

first time she'd ever seen him, she'd noticed how smoothly he moved. It must be because of all the dancing he'd done as part of The Zig-Zaggers.

'I'm sorry,' she said as she straightened.

'"*Sorry*"? This . . .' Mr Hawkins held the frame protectively in front of his stomach, where it couldn't be glimpsed through the glass windows of the office. '. . . this is *private*. Personal! You had no business snooping through my things!'

'You're right,' Ivy said, stepping away from the desk. 'And I am sorry. But I also really don't understand.' She shook her head. 'Why have you been keeping your band a secret? Why don't you have this cover up on the wall with your other posters?'

'Are you kidding?' Shuddering, Mr Hawkins pushed past her to shove the frame back into its hiding place and slam the drawer closed. 'If anyone else finds out . . .' He cringed and sank down on to the chair behind the desk. 'Thank goodness I

186

didn't use my real name in the band, so no one can find me by searching online. If those students –' he waved at the windows – 'ever found out that I used to sing songs with ridiculous titles . . .'

'Like what?' Ivy asked.

'Never mind,' he muttered, closing his eyes.

Ivy crossed her arms. 'Come on, Mr Hawkins. They couldn't have been *that* band.'

'Oh no?' Mr Hawkins opened his eyes and scowled at her. 'Well, what do you think of this, then? Our second biggest hit was a song called "C-C-C-C-C-Clean Up Your Room!"'

Ivy felt a snort-laugh coming. She slammed one hand up to her face to hold it back. 'We-e-e-ell . . .'

Mr Hawkins's own mouth twitched into a reluctant smile. 'And better yet . . . our biggest hit was "Victorious Victor Vacuum!"'

'No!' Ivy couldn't keep back her laughter any more. 'I don't believe it.'

'Believe it.' He was grinning openly now.

'Although I always personally preferred "Marvellous Molly Mop" . . .'

'That's fantastic.' Ivy shook her head, still laughing. 'But seriously. You actually made a living from your music – something that musicians all over the world struggle to do. You should be proud!'

Mr Hawkins gave a sarcastic laugh. Then he shrugged and leaned back in his seat. 'Yeah, we made a living. But it wasn't a challenge. And how many musicians really dream of growing up to wear a fuzzy orange wig on stage?' He gave a short, humourless laugh. 'Look, I'm not some precious *artiste*, or anything, but the truth is, I have talent. I can sing, I can dance, I can play every instrument in that room . . .' He pointed to the music room next door. '. . . and I can play even more instruments that this school can't afford to buy. Have you ever heard of a theramin?'

'Um . . .' Ivy shrugged.

188

'Exactly!' He pointed at her triumphantly. 'Well, I can play it so well it would make you cry!'

'Then why don't you show us?' Ivy said gently. 'Mr Hawkins, it's no good hiding the truth about yourself. No one should ever choose to do that.' *And I know all about it!* she added silently. 'You can't let people think you were some rock god. The truth *will* come out eventually, no matter how you try to hide it, and if you wait until someone else finds out then everyone will be really mad. But if you're honest and upfront about it now . . .' She shrugged. 'Well, I guess some people might be shocked. But in the end, they'll respect you for it. And you won't have to keep all those secrets any more.'

There was a long moment of silence in the tiny office, as guitars wailed in the room next door. Finally, Mr Hawkins sat forwards in his seat. 'You're right,' he said quietly. Leaning down, he pulled the frame back out of his desk drawer and set it carefully on top of the piles of sheet music that covered his desk. 'It's better to be a Zig-Zagger forever . . . than it is to be a fake.' Sighing, he looked up at Ivy. 'You know what? You're wise beyond your years, young lady. I've been so worried about people discovering who I really am, I pretended to be someone I am really, really not. And that's no way to live. I feel better already . . .'

Ivy only gave him a small smile as she turned to leave the room. *Yeah, I'm wise, but you don't know the half of it. If you knew the Bigger Problems that my family were dealing with . . .*

When she left the room, the only thing on her mind was her sister. Now that the school mystery had been solved, it was time to resume worrying about Olivia and Jackson.

Olivia held Jackson's hand as they sat down that night at the long table in the familiar meeting room at ASHH. Outside night had fallen, but inside the room, Ms Deborg showed no signs of tiredness as she held her binder open before her and gave a lecture that seemed it would never end.

'. . . And so this third and final Test is the *Test of Blood*. It is the culmination of all of your previous challenges. It will be your toughest challenge so far!'

'Um . . .' Jackson's hand tightened around Olivia's and he gave an audible gulp. 'I don't have to, like . . . *drink* something, do I?'

Ms Deborg smirked as she looked past him to Olivia. 'Humans *always* make that assumption.'

Oops. Olivia flushed as she remembered making the same mistake on her own Third Test. Ms Deborg had been just as withering in her response then, too. Her remembered words made Olivia's shoulders hunch with embarrassment all over again.

'*That would be a Test of Fortitude, wouldn't it?*'

The secretary didn't make the same correction

this time, but the smirk deepened on her face as she turned back to Jackson. 'In fact,' she murmured, 'the Test of Blood is a very simple one.'

Oh, thank goodness. Olivia felt a shiver of pure relief as she recognised that wording. *This is going exactly the same way as my Test!* It might actually be easy after all. All that Jackson would have to do was swear the Blood Oath and allow his finger to be pricked so that a drop of his blood would hit parchment, and then . . .

'*Your* Test will be a very straightforward question,' purred Ms Deborg. 'Are you prepared to give up your family for the vampire community? *For Olivia?*'

Olivia gasped in horror, dropping Jackson's hand. She had definitely relaxed too soon.

Chapter Ten

Even as the gasp broke out of Olivia's mouth, Jackson was already shaking his head violently. 'You can't be serious!'

Ms Deborg's smirk didn't falter as she gave him a single, solemn nod. 'When it comes to matters of vampire security, Mr Caulfield, I am never less than *deadly* serious.'

'But –!' Jackson gawped at her. 'You'd seriously demand that I just turn my back on my family?'

Ms Deborg's gaze intensified. 'So is that where your true loyalty lies? With your blood relatives? I see . . .' She looked down at the binder in front of her, picking up a pen and holding it above the page.

It was a small gesture, but to Olivia, it seemed so . . . *final*.

'I . . . I . . .' Jackson looked from Olivia to the secretary and back again, clearly panicked.

Olivia didn't need her twin's vamp powers to hear his heart pounding in his chest. Her own heart was slamming against hers in sorrow.

'This is so unfair,' she whispered.

No one forced me to make that choice. Why should Jackson have to give up his family just so that he could be with her?

'I told you this final Test would be difficult,' Ms Deborg murmured, pen still hovering above the page. 'In fact, I personally find it . . . revelatory.'

Olivia had gone numb with shock. Jackson just stared at her. He did not make a move to reach out, hold her hand. They were standing only two feet apart, but it might as well have been two miles.

She glimpsed tears in his blue eyes. 'I'm so sorry, Olivia,' he whispered. 'I love you.' His shoulders stiffened as he swivelled around to glower at Ms Deborg. 'But I can *never* turn my back on my blood relatives. Who do you even think you are to make that kind of demand of me?'

He stuck out his jaw, his glare burning. 'If you've separated families in the past just so you can keep your stupid secret – and frankly, drinking blood isn't even half as weird as some of the things I've heard of other actors in Hollywood doing when they're not on set! – then the truth is vamps aren't just bloodsuckers. They flat-out *suck!*'

Olivia closed her eyes and let her tears slide down her face as his words rang through the room. She couldn't understand how she could feel such sadness at losing him, at the same time as feeling so proud of him for standing up to the vamps.

Jackson had just failed the Third Test ... and the worst part was, she couldn't even blame him.

Who would give up their whole family? If

she'd been given that test, she would have made the same decision.

'Jackson's right,' she said. 'That's just unreasonable.'

But she couldn't help reaching for his hand, one last time, clenching her fingers tightly around his. Maybe when she got home, if she called her grandparents right away, they might be willing to get involved, to help her. Maybe, if the VRT waited just a few days for their mindwipe thing . . .

No, she thought hollowly. *There's nothing we can do now. This is the last time I'll ever hold his hand. The last time he'll feel any love for me.*

The sound of Ms Deborg's slow chuckle made her eyes fly open. 'You're laughing?' Olivia demanded. She lurched to her feet, fury rushing through her, and slammed her hands down on the table. 'I don't believe it. How can you look so *smug* when you've just ruined everything?'

'Oh, Olivia.' Ms Deborg shook her head

slowly. 'You don't understand at all, do you? Your boyfriend has just passed the Third Test.'

'*What?*' Olivia's gaze flew to Jackson's face. He looked just as stunned as she felt.

'I don't understand either,' he whispered.

'No?' Ms Deborg smiled as she rose to her feet. 'You have proven that you understand the bonds of blood. By firmly, and without hesitation, vowing never to forsake your family, you have proven that you are naturally honourable at heart, and you *can*, after all, be trusted by the Vampire Round Table.' She closed the binder with a *thunk*. 'Congratulations, Mr Caulfield. You have passed all Three Tests, and the Blood Secret is yours to keep.'

🦇   🦇   🦇

I'm so glad everything worked out, Ivy thought. She was sitting with Olivia outside the ASHH office. It had been two days since Jackson had passed the Three Tests, proving he could keep the Blood Secret, and her twin was showing her a text message from him, saying that he was back home, and that all the Hollywood vamps knew he had passed.

They're being even nicer to me now, he wrote. *They're even talking about putting me in a musical!*

Ivy laughed, peering at her sister. 'I didn't know Jackson could sing and dance.'

Olivia cringed. 'He's not as great as he thinks he is,' she chuckled. 'But you know he'll take *all* the lessons he'll need to get great at it.'

Ivy grinned at her, then pointed at the ASHH office. 'I bet you're just "thrilled" to be back here, huh?' she said sarcastically.

Olivia rolled her eyes. 'No way. I'm *really* not looking forward to seeing Ms Deborg again.' She grimaced. 'That woman's sense of humour is a nightmare!'

'Yes, but at least you don't have to worry about it any more.' Ivy wrapped one arm around her twin, tipping her head against Olivia's.

'That's true,' Olivia agreed fervently. 'I'm just

relieved there's no more secrets. Honestly, keeping the vamp secret from Jackson totally *bit*!'

Ivy let out a startled laugh at the pun and Olivia joined in . . . but their laughter died all too soon as the security guard nearby cleared his throat and the reality of the situation flooded in.

'This time, we're here for me,' Ivy said quietly. She pulled her arm back from her twin's shoulders to lace both hands in her lap. 'Because *I'm* the problem.'

'It's not a problem,' Olivia said firmly. 'The fact that you've developed your ninth sense early is amazing! Dad says it's really impressive, remember?'

'Yeah, but what's the VRT going to do about it?' Ivy whispered. 'It may sound cool to be a "special" vampire . . . but what if they end up sending me somewhere like Wallachia Academy to learn how to control it better?' She twisted her hands in her lap. 'I can't stand to be sent away from my family *again*.'

Olivia's face tightened. 'Then we won't let that happen.'

Ivy jerked her shoulders in an unhappy shrug. 'Every time I think I'm safe at home with you guys, something like this happens.'

'Well . . .' Olivia sighed. 'I hate to say it, Ivy, but it's true: you really are a special vampire!' She winked. 'I bet your truth-sense didn't go off when I said that, did it?'

Ivy narrowed her eyes. 'Are you actually teasing me about my truth-sense right now?'

'That's what sisters are for,' Olivia said primly. Then she laughed. 'Seriously, though, sis: do you think we'll always face this kind of challenge?'

'Maybe,' Ivy said, squeezing her sister's hand tight. 'But the only thing that really matters is that we face all our challenges together.'

The door to ASHH slid open.

Valencia Deborg stood in the doorway, wearing a killer dark blue kimono with a fabulous blood-red sunset painted across it. 'Well, Miss Vega?' The secretary arched one high, plucked eyebrow. 'Are you ready?'

With her sister at her side, Ivy rose to her feet. 'Yes,' she said quietly. 'I'm ready.'

Her truth-sense didn't even quiver at her own words.

It's true, she realised. *I wasn't fibbing – I really am ready for whatever the VRT has to throw at me!*

Looking at Olivia's determined face, she found herself smiling.

And of course she was smiling. After all, for over a year, she'd known she was a vampire with a bunny twin . . . so being "special" and "unique" was kind of old news to her now!

Holding her twin's warm hand, Ivy stepped through the doorway without looking back.

TWIN TALK!

A fangtastic winter treat for you, as VAMP magazine's Georgia Huntingdon checks in with our favourite twins, at the end of another amazing semester!

Georgia: So, guys, how was your very first semester of high school?

Ivy: Oh, gosh, so much has happened, I barely remember anything about actual school. Is that bad?

Olivia: Only if you want to pass your exams.

Georgia: I think you can be forgiven.

Ivy: Yeah, I mean – we had to deal with the loss of a priceless vampire heirloom, a 'ghost-grabber', and Jackson learning the Blood Secret. So many distractions!

Olivia: But if anyone can stake all the problems in front of them, it's Ivy Vega!

Georgia: Olivia, you've just returned from more filming days on your movie. How was that?

Olivia: Super-fun! It's going really, really well – Jackson and I were in a town called Pine Wood. We saw an old classmate of ours – Debi Morgan. She moved there over summer. It was nice to catch up, but . . .

Georgia: But what?

Olivia: I don't know. There was something a bit strange about Pine Wood. I couldn't put my finger on it.

Ivy: Don't worry, sis. I checked before you left – there's no vamp community in that town.

Olivia: It was definitely spooky, though. Maybe there were, like, ghosts or werewolves, or something?

Ivy: (laughs): There's no such thing as werewolves!

Olivia: Isn't that what most people think about vamps?

Ivy: Huh . . . I guess you're right . . .